Love Beyond Time

A Tale of Fate, Love, and Destiny

This is a work of fiction. Names, characters, places, and incidents either are the product of the author's imagination or are used fictitiously. Any resemblance to actual persons, living or dead, events, or locales is entirely coincidental.

ISBN: 978-93-342-3725-2

Written by Divyam Agarwal
Cover Design by: Divyam Agarwal

Published by: Self-Published

Printed in India

For information about special discounts for bulk purchases, please contact the author at contact@divyamagarwal.com

Why "**Love Beyond Time**"?

Love is not just a feeling; it is a force that transcends time, space, and even fate itself. *Love Beyond Time* is a story that explores the idea that true love never fades—it lingers in the echoes of the past, waiting to be rediscovered. Set against the backdrop of colonial India and modern times, this tale follows Anika, who stumbles upon a forgotten love story buried in the walls of an old haveli. As she unravels the mystery, she finds herself drawn into the past, where love and destiny intertwine in ways beyond imagination. This is not just a romance—it is proof that when two souls are meant to be together, not even time can keep them apart.

Plot Overview:

Love Beyond Time is a mesmerizing tale of love, loss, and destiny set against the historical charm of colonial India and the vibrant modern era. The story follows **Anika**, a young historian who moves into an ancestral **haveli** in Kolkata, a property that has been in her family for generations but has remained abandoned for decades. As she settles into the grand yet eerie mansion, she stumbles upon a set of old love letters hidden in the walls. These letters, written in the 1920s, reveal a heart-wrenching romance between **Aarav**, a gifted painter, and **Meera**, a poet whose love was torn apart by unknown circumstances.

Anika, drawn to the passion and sorrow within these letters, becomes obsessed with uncovering the mystery behind their fate. However, as she digs deeper, strange occurrences begin—faint whispers in empty hallways, flickering lights, and, most shockingly, moments where she finds herself transported back in time to 1925. In the past, she comes face-to-face with **Aarav**, a man who inexplicably recognizes something in her, as though they have met before.

As Anika's visits to the past become more frequent, she finds herself falling for Aarav, despite knowing she is

Why "**Love Beyond Time**"?

Love is not just a feeling; it is a force that transcends time, space, and even fate itself. *Love Beyond Time* is a story that explores the idea that true love never fades—it lingers in the echoes of the past, waiting to be rediscovered. Set against the backdrop of colonial India and modern times, this tale follows Anika, who stumbles upon a forgotten love story buried in the walls of an old haveli. As she unravels the mystery, she finds herself drawn into the past, where love and destiny intertwine in ways beyond imagination. This is not just a romance—it is proof that when two souls are meant to be together, not even time can keep them apart.

Plot Overview:

Love Beyond Time is a mesmerizing tale of love, loss, and destiny set against the historical charm of colonial India and the vibrant modern era. The story follows **Anika**, a young historian who moves into an ancestral **haveli** in Kolkata, a property that has been in her family for generations but has remained abandoned for decades. As she settles into the grand yet eerie mansion, she stumbles upon a set of old love letters hidden in the walls. These letters, written in the 1920s, reveal a heart-wrenching romance between **Aarav**, a gifted painter, and **Meera**, a poet whose love was torn apart by unknown circumstances.

Anika, drawn to the passion and sorrow within these letters, becomes obsessed with uncovering the mystery behind their fate. However, as she digs deeper, strange occurrences begin—faint whispers in empty hallways, flickering lights, and, most shockingly, moments where she finds herself transported back in time to 1925. In the past, she comes face-to-face with **Aarav**, a man who inexplicably recognizes something in her, as though they have met before.

As Anika's visits to the past become more frequent, she finds herself falling for Aarav, despite knowing she is merely a visitor in his world. Torn between her growing love and the need to protect history from being altered, she begins to uncover the truth about **Meera's tragic fate** and **Aarav's sudden disappearance** from all records. But fate is a cruel master, and the more she intervenes, the closer she gets to realizing that she might be the reason why Aarav vanished in the first place.

Now, she faces an impossible choice—stay in the past and risk rewriting history or return to her time and let their love remain a forgotten memory. But love, when true, never fades. As Anika wakes up in the present, believing everything to be a dream, she discovers something impossible—a **painting of herself**, signed by Aarav in 1925. Decades later, she meets **Ishaan**, a young artist who resembles Aarav, carrying a legacy neither of them fully understands. In the end, love proves to be timeless, finding its way across centuries, waiting for the right moment to bloom once more.

Key Themes:

Timeless Love: The story challenges the notion that love is confined to a single lifetime. Anika and Aarav's love transcends generations, proving that some bonds never break, no matter how much time passes.

Destiny vs. Free Will: The novel explores whether fate is already written or if choices can alter history. Anika's journey forces her to question whether she is truly in control of her actions or merely a pawn in a preordained destiny.

The Power of Memories: The letters, the paintings, and the old haveli serve as vessels of memory, proving that love stories, even those forgotten by history, leave behind echoes.

Sacrifice and Redemption: Love often requires painful sacrifices. Anika must decide between staying with Aarav and preserving the timeline. Meera's past decisions also hold a key to understanding what truly happened to Aarav.

History and Identity: As Anika uncovers her family's hidden past, she realizes that history is not just about facts—it is about emotions, people, and the stories that shape who we become.

Plot Structure:

Exposition: Anika moves into the old haveli, unaware of the secrets buried within its walls.

Inciting Incident: She finds the letters and experiences her first encounter with the past.

Rising Action: She meets Aarav in 1925, uncovering the truth about his love for Meera.

Climax: Anika realizes that she is responsible for Aarav's disappearance, forcing her to make a devastating choice.

Falling Action: She wakes up in the present, believing the past has slipped away, only to find a final message from Aarav.

Resolution: She meets Ishaan, proof that love never truly disappears—it just finds a new form.

Character Development:

Anika Sharma (The Present-Day Historian): At the beginning, Anika is a rational, logical woman who believes in facts over emotions. As she uncovers the love story of the past, she becomes more in tune with her heart, realizing that history is not just about events but about emotions, connections, and the lives that shaped them.

Aarav Malhotra (The 1925 Painter): A passionate artist with an old soul, Aarav is deeply in love with Meera. As he encounters Anika, he senses something eerily familiar about her. His struggle with societal expectations and his mysterious disappearance shape the heart of the story.

Meera Bose (The 1925 Poet): Meera is the key to the entire mystery. Through her poetry and letters, Anika pieces together the truth about Aarav's past. Meera's love was deep, yet something forced them apart, leading to Aarav's erasure from history.

Ishaan Malhotra (The Modern-Day Artist): A rising painter in Mumbai, Ishaan is Aarav's great-grandson. He carries an artistic legacy that he does not fully understand until he meets Anika. Their meeting suggests that love, though lost in one lifetime, always finds a way back.

Symbolism:

The Haveli: The mansion represents time itself, holding memories within its walls, waiting to be rediscovered.

The Letters: They bridge the past and present, carrying emotions that refuse to be forgotten.

The Painting of Meera: Aarav's way of keeping love alive even when it is lost. Later, when Anika discovers a painting of herself, it proves that love can defy time.

The Clock Stopping at Midnight: Every night before Anika slips into the past, the clock in the haveli freezes at midnight—marking the exact moment history was altered.

Emotional Impact:

The novel takes the reader on a deeply emotional journey—one filled with longing, nostalgia, and heartbreak. There is an ache in knowing that some love stories never find a happy ending in the way we expect, yet the beauty lies in the fact that love, in its truest form, is never truly lost. The reader will feel Anika's pain as she falls for someone who belongs to another time and experience the bittersweet joy of realizing that love always finds a way, even if in a different form or lifetime.

The novel is not just a romance—it is a reflection of how love weaves itself into history, waiting for the right soul to rediscover it.

Ending Notes:

The ending of *Love Beyond Time* is both haunting and hopeful. Anika, believing she has left the past behind, finds a **painting of herself**, signed by Aarav in 1925—a clear sign that he remembered her even after she disappeared from his timeline. This discovery shakes her to the core, proving that she was not merely dreaming but truly lived in another time.

Years later, at an art exhibition, she meets **Ishaan Malhotra**, Aarav's great-grandson, who looks eerily similar to the painter she once loved. Their meeting hints that perhaps Aarav's love lived on through his lineage, finding its way back to Anika in another lifetime. Love is not bound by time—it is simply waiting for the right moment to return.

Table of Contents

The Forgotten Haveli

Anika arrives in Kolkata to restore her ancestral haveli, a mansion abandoned for decades. As she steps inside, a strange sense of familiarity washes over her, even though she has never been here before. The air is thick with whispers of the past, and something about the place unsettles her. While exploring the dusty corridors, she stumbles upon a hidden chamber containing a box filled with old letters—letters that seem to hold a love story lost in time. But whose story is it? And why does she feel so drawn to it?

The rhythmic chug of the train had been soothing, but as the wheels screeched to a halt at **Howrah Station**, Anika jolted awake, her heart pounding with an unshakable mix of excitement and nervousness. The air was thick with the scent of damp earth, hot tea, and the distant aroma of fried snacks from nearby stalls. A cool breeze carried the sounds of hawkers calling out their wares, rickshaw bells clanging, and the endless chatter of travelers bustling through the station.

She tightened her grip on her bag and stepped onto the platform, adjusting the dupatta draped over her shoulder. Kolkata—the city her grandmother had spoken of with a strange mix of nostalgia and sorrow. A city that had been her family's home for generations, yet one she had never truly known.

Outside, the chaos of the city welcomed her. Yellow taxis honked impatiently, vendors shouted prices of fresh-cut fruits, and an old man sat at a corner, skillfully sketching portraits of passersby. It was as if time coexisted in layers here—colonial-era buildings stood tall beside modern glass towers, while trams still rumbled through the roads as if refusing to be forgotten.

She approached a line of taxis and hesitated for a moment before telling the driver her destination.

"**Rajbari Haveli, Baghbazar**," she said, testing the words on her tongue.

The driver, an elderly man with graying hair, turned to look at her, his eyes narrowing slightly. A moment of hesitation flickered across his face before he nodded and started the engine.

"You're going to the old haveli?" he asked, as they weaved through the streets.

"Yes," she replied. "It belonged to my family."

The driver let out a slow breath. "It has been abandoned for years, hasn't it?"

Anika nodded, staring out the window as the city blurred past her. She had read about the haveli in family records, seen faded photographs, but no one had lived there since her great-grandfather's time. And yet, something about the place had called to her. She couldn't explain it, but she had felt drawn to it ever since she learned it still stood, waiting.

After what felt like an eternity, the taxi pulled up in front of the haveli.

Anika stepped out and gazed at the **majestic yet decaying structure** before her. The **Rajbari Haveli** stood like a forgotten relic of time, its once-white walls now covered in patches of moss, cracked paint, and creeping ivy. The intricate wooden carvings on the main doors were faded but still bore the craftsmanship of a bygone era. The iron gates groaned as she pushed them open, revealing an overgrown **courtyard**. Fallen leaves crunched beneath her feet as she moved forward, her heart thudding with an unfamiliar anticipation.

She glanced up at the towering structure. Balconies with ornate railings loomed over her, the windows dark and empty, like watchful eyes. The air was heavy, carrying the scent of old wood, damp stone, and something else—a faint fragrance of **sandalwood and roses**, as if time itself had preserved the essence of those who had once lived here.

As she walked through the open doorway, dust swirled in the air, disturbed by her presence. The **grand hallway** stretched before her, its marble floors covered in layers of forgotten time. The walls were adorned with **portraits of ancestors**, their eyes seeming to follow her as she moved. Chandeliers hung from the high ceiling, their crystals dull with dust but still holding traces of their former grandeur.

She ran her fingers along the wooden railing of the **staircase**, its carvings intricate despite years of neglect. A sudden **gust of wind** rushed through the halls, rattling the windows, and a door creaked open on its own. Anika' s breath hitched.

Summoning courage, she stepped inside what appeared to be an old study. The shelves stretched from floor to ceiling, filled with books covered in cobwebs. The wooden desk near the window was coated in dust, but something about it felt untouched, waiting.

Then she saw it.

A **mahogany trunk** tucked away in the corner, its brass lock slightly rusted but still intact. She moved towards it, her fingers trembling as she unlatched it. The lid creaked open, revealing a bundle of old **letters** tied together with a faded silk ribbon. The paper was yellowed with age, the ink slightly smudged, yet the writing remained clear.

Her heartbeat quickened as she pulled out the first letter. The date at the top read **1925**.

A strange sensation washed over her—**déjà vu**, as if she had held these letters before, as if she had read these words in another lifetime. Her fingers traced the elegant handwriting, her breath catching as she read the opening lines.

"My dearest Meera," the letter began.

Meera.

Who was she? And why did Anika feel an inexplicable connection to the name?

As she continued reading, something strange happened. The room around her blurred, the walls flickering between light and shadow. The scent of sandalwood and roses intensified, wrapping around her like a memory she couldn't grasp. And for a brief moment, she felt as though she was no longer in the present, but somewhere else entirely.

Somewhere in **1925**.

The Letter from the Past

Anika begins reading the old letters, discovering the poetic words of a man deeply in love with a woman named Meera. The letter feels strangely personal, as if written not just for someone in the past but for her as well. As she reads on, a wave of dizziness overtakes her, and suddenly, she finds herself in another time—Kolkata, 1925. Confused and disoriented, she watches as a young man with an artist' s soul writes the very letter she had just been holding. But how is this possible? Is she dreaming, or has she truly stepped into the past?

Anika's fingers trembled as she traced the words on the fragile sheet of paper. The ink, though faded with age, still carried the weight of longing.

"My dearest Meera,
Every brushstroke of my paintings is filled with you, every color I choose reminds me of your eyes, your laughter, the way the morning light catches in your hair. The world is a beautiful place, but none of it compares to you. My heart belongs to you, in this life and beyond.
—Aarav"

Aarav. Meera. Their names stirred something deep inside her. She read the letter again, her heart racing. Who were these lovers lost in time? And why did the words feel so··· familiar?

The room around her suddenly felt smaller, as if the walls were closing in. A faint ringing filled her ears, and the candle on the old wooden desk flickered unnaturally. The air thickened, and for a moment, she struggled to breathe.

Then, everything shifted.

The dusty shelves, the cracked walls, the dim light of the abandoned haveli—all of it faded like mist. A rush of warmth surrounded her, the scent of fresh jasmine filling the air. The room she had been standing in was no longer abandoned; it was alive, vibrant, full of color.

She gasped.

Before her stood a **young man**, dressed in an elegant white kurta, his sleeves rolled up, his dark hair falling over his forehead as he leaned over a **wooden desk**, penning the very letter she had just been reading. His ink-stained fingers moved gracefully, pausing every now and then as if he were lost in thought.

The soft glow of an **oil lamp** flickered beside him, casting a warm light across the room. The **walls**, once covered in dust, were now decorated with fresh paintings—portraits, landscapes, emotions captured on canvas with an artist's delicate touch. The wooden bookshelves stood proudly, filled with neatly arranged volumes.

Anika felt her breath catch in her throat.

How was this possible?

She took an uncertain step forward, but the **wooden floor did not creak** beneath her weight. The young man—Aarav—did not notice her presence. It was as if she were merely a shadow, an observer trapped between two times.

Her mind raced. Had she lost consciousness? Was she dreaming? Or had she truly··· stepped into the past?

Aarav finished the letter with a final stroke, sealing it in an envelope with **careful precision**. He lifted it gently, bringing it close to his chest for a fleeting moment before placing it inside a **small wooden box** on his desk. His expression was one of quiet yearning, of a love too deep for words.

Then, a voice called from outside the room.

"Aarav?"

Anika turned toward the doorway, and for the first time, she saw her.

Meera.

She was breathtaking, dressed in a simple but elegant **cotton saree**, the color of the early morning sky. Her dark eyes held a quiet depth, her long hair cascading down her back in soft waves. She walked toward Aarav with familiarity, with warmth, as if her presence in his space was as natural as the air he breathed.

"You're still writing?" she asked, a soft smile playing on her lips.

Aarav looked up, his entire face lighting up at the sight of her. "How could I not? When you leave, it feels as though the whole world turns silent."

Meera chuckled, shaking her head. "You and your words. What will you do if I stop visiting?"

Aarav leaned back, crossing his arms. "Then I suppose I'll have to paint a thousand portraits of you, just to keep your presence alive in this room."

Anika watched the exchange with wide eyes. Their love was tangible, almost sacred. The way Aarav looked at Meera—like she was the very essence of his existence—sent shivers down her spine.

Meera walked to the window, looking out at the moonlit courtyard. "You know my father will never approve of us," she said softly, the weight of reality creeping into her voice.

Aarav stood, walking toward her. "Does that mean we stop loving each other?"

Meera turned to face him, her expression conflicted. "No··· but love alone is not always enough, Aarav."

A shadow passed over his face, but he did not argue. Instead, he reached for her hand, tracing soft circles against her palm. "Then tell me what is enough, Meera. Because I have spent my life painting the world, and yet no color has ever held meaning until I found you."

Anika felt something tighten in her chest. This was real. This was love—the kind that defied time, that clung to existence even when the world stood against it.

And yet, she knew how these stories often ended.

The weight of history, the tragedy of lovers separated by time and fate—it loomed over her like an unspoken warning.

Suddenly, the room began to fade, dissolving into shadows. The voices softened, growing distant.

Anika gasped as she was pulled backward, as if some invisible force was dragging her through time itself.

Then—

She was back.

The **dusty study** returned, the light dim once more. The paintings were gone. The wooden box on the desk now sat covered in cobwebs, untouched for decades. The air was heavy, but it was no longer filled with the scent of jasmine and oil lamps.

The past had let her go.

Anika clutched the letter in her hand, her mind spinning. She had seen them. She had heard their voices, felt the weight of their love.

But how?

Tears stung her eyes as she whispered their names.

"Aarav and Meera⋯"

Somehow, she knew—this was just the beginning.

Somewhere, buried beneath the dust of time, their story was waiting to be uncovered.

The Mystery Deepens

Anika struggles to make sense of what just happened. Did she really travel to the past, or was it just her imagination playing tricks on her? As she searches for answers, she finds more letters hidden inside the wooden box—each one revealing more about Aarav and Meera's love story. But something feels unfinished, as if their story was never completed. Determined to uncover the truth, Anika starts digging into the history of the haveli, unaware that the past is not done with her yet.

Anika sat motionless, gripping the old letter in her trembling hands. The room around her was the same—dusty, abandoned, frozen in time—but **something within her had changed**.

She had been there. She had seen Aarav writing the letter, had felt the weight of Meera's presence in the room. It wasn't a dream. It couldn't be. The emotions, the voices, the warmth of the oil lamp—it had been too real.

Her mind raced.

"Is this even possible?" she whispered to herself, her voice barely audible in the empty study.

She turned her gaze back to the **wooden box** on the desk. Her fingers trembled as she lifted the lid, dust scattering into the air. Inside, a neat stack of **old letters** lay tied together with a faded silk ribbon.

Anika's heart pounded. If one letter had pulled her into the past, what would the others reveal?

Carefully, she untied the ribbon and picked up the next letter. The paper was delicate, threatening to crumble at her touch. She unfolded it slowly, her eyes scanning the handwritten words.

"My love,
The world sees me as a painter, but they do not know that you are my muse. Every color I choose, every brushstroke I make, is my way of holding you close. The walls may separate us, but our hearts beat as one. I dream of the day when we will no longer have to meet in secret, when I can hold your hand under the open sky without fear. But until then, my love, I will paint you into every sunset, every dream, every moment of my life."

Anika swallowed hard. This was more than just a love story. There was longing here, pain buried between the lines. Aarav and Meera had been forced to hide their love.

"Why?" she murmured, flipping the letter over, hoping to find more clues. But there was nothing—just his name, written in elegant script.

A sudden gust of wind blew through the broken window, causing the candle on the desk to flicker. Anika shivered. **The air felt different.**

She turned back to the box, her fingers brushing against something harder than paper. Pushing aside the stack of letters, she found **a small, leather-bound diary** tucked beneath them. The cover was cracked with age, the edges worn down.

Her pulse quickened as she opened it.

The pages were filled with **sketches**—beautiful, haunting portraits of Meera. Some were quick, hurried sketches, capturing fleeting moments of joy. Others were **detailed, intricate pieces**, as if Aarav had spent hours trying to perfect every delicate feature of her face.

Anika flipped through the pages, her breath catching as she reached one particular drawing.

It was of **Meera**, standing by a window, staring at the moon. But something about this one felt different. The way her shoulders were slumped, the sadness in her eyes—this wasn't just a simple portrait.

There was **pain** in this image. A silent sorrow woven into every line of the drawing.

Anika's heart ached for them. Whatever had happened to Aarav and Meera, it hadn't been simple.

She closed the diary gently, her thoughts swirling.

"I need to know what happened to them."

She had to dig deeper.

A Trip to the Archives

The next morning, Anika found herself at the **Kolkata Historical Archives**, a vast library filled with ancient records, newspapers, and documents that chronicled the city's past.

The librarian, an elderly man with silver-rimmed glasses, gave her a curious look as she explained her request.

"You're looking for information on the old Bose Haveli?" he asked, adjusting his glasses.

Anika nodded. "Yes. I recently visited the place and found some old letters. I think they belonged to a man named Aarav."

The librarian's expression changed slightly, a flicker of recognition in his eyes. He didn't speak immediately, but after a pause, he stood up and motioned for her to follow.

"This way," he said, leading her to a section of **old newspaper records**.

As Anika sifted through the fragile sheets, her fingers brushing against history itself, she finally stumbled upon a **headline that made her blood run cold**.

"Tragedy Strikes Bose Haveli: Young Painter Disappears Without a Trace."

Her heart pounded as she read further.

"Aarav Malhotra, a promising young artist, mysteriously vanished from his residence at Bose Haveli in the year 1925. Friends and family reported that he was last seen working in his study late at night. No signs of forced entry or struggle were found. To this day, his disappearance remains an unsolved mystery."

Anika's hands shook.

"He vanished?"

She read the article again, hoping to find more details, but the report ended abruptly. No explanations. No closure.

Just a young artist lost to time.

She leaned back in her chair, her mind spinning. If Aarav had disappeared, what had happened to Meera?

She quickly searched through the remaining newspapers, flipping pages with urgency. But there was nothing—no mention of Meera, no follow-up articles, nothing to explain what had become of them.

A heavy silence settled over her.

Aarav's love letters, his paintings, the longing in his words—it had all led to this. A sudden disappearance. An unfinished story.

And somehow, **she was a part of it now**.

The Past Calls Again

That night, back at the haveli, Anika sat by the desk, the old letters spread out before her. The weight of history pressed down on her.

"What happened to you, Aarav?" she whispered, running her fingers over his handwriting.

She stared at the candle's flickering flame, her thoughts clouded with questions.

Then, a familiar sensation washed over her.

The air thickened. The walls seemed to blur. The floor beneath her feet faded.

Her breath caught.

It was happening again.

The past wasn't done with her yet.

And this time, she was ready.

A Glimpse of the Past

Anika finds herself slipping into the past once more, drawn deeper into the world of 1925. This time, she is not just a spectator—she feels the emotions, the air, the weight of the time she is stepping into. As she stands in the same haveli, now alive with the echoes of history, she comes face to face with Aarav and Meera. But something about this moment feels different. Is she merely witnessing their story, or is she becoming a part of it?

Anika barely had time to process what was happening. One moment, she was in the cold, abandoned study of the haveli, surrounded by old letters and forgotten memories. The next, the air around her shimmered, bending and twisting like ripples on the surface of water.

Her vision blurred. The candlelight flickered wildly. The old wooden desk, the peeling walls, the broken window—they all **shifted.**

And then, **she was no longer in the present.**

The air was warm, filled with the rich scent of sandalwood and burning oil lamps. The dusty silence of the abandoned room was replaced by the **gentle hum of**

voices, the faint rustling of fabric, the soft echo of footsteps on polished floors.

Anika's heart pounded as she turned around.

The haveli was **alive.**

The cracked walls were restored, gleaming under the golden light of chandeliers. Heavy silk curtains swayed gently with the evening breeze. The desk that had once been covered in dust and forgotten letters was now **neatly arranged**, with ink bottles, quills, and parchment paper scattered across its surface.

And sitting at that desk, his head bent over a canvas, was **Aarav.**

Anika inhaled sharply.

He was real. Not just a name on a letter, not just an idea or a sketch. **A man of flesh and blood, breathing, living.**

His long fingers moved carefully, dipping the brush into a pot of paint before dragging it across the canvas with precision. His dark hair fell slightly over his forehead, his brow furrowed in deep concentration. A small oil lamp flickered beside him, casting shadows that danced across the walls.

For a moment, Anika forgot to breathe.

This wasn't a dream. **She was truly here.**

She took a hesitant step forward, half-expecting the world around her to shatter like glass. But nothing changed. The past **held onto her**.

A soft voice suddenly broke the silence.

"Aarav, how long will you keep painting?"

Anika turned towards the doorway.

Meera stood there, dressed in a simple but elegant saree, her bangles softly clinking as she stepped closer. Her hair was loosely tied back, a few strands escaping to frame her delicate face. There was warmth in her eyes, but also something else—**a quiet sadness, a longing that she tried to hide.**

Aarav looked up, his expression softening. "Just a little longer, Meera."

"You say that every night," Meera teased, walking over to him. She peered at the painting, her lips curving into a smile. "Another portrait?"

Aarav chuckled. "I can't help it. Every time I try to paint something else, my hands find their way back to you."

Meera blushed, shaking her head. "What will the world say if they see how much of your time you waste on me?"

"They'll say I was a fool," Aarav said, reaching out to tuck a loose strand of hair behind her ear. "And they'll be right. Because no matter how much I paint you, it will never be enough."

Anika's chest tightened. She could **feel** the love between them, the unspoken promises in their gaze.

But underneath it all, there was something else—**a shadow of sorrow, a tension that neither of them dared to voice.**

Anika took another step closer, drawn to their conversation. But as she moved, **the wooden floor beneath her creaked.**

Aarav's head snapped up.

His gaze locked onto hers.

Anika **froze.**

For the first time since she had slipped into the past, someone was looking **directly at her.**

The Breaking of Time

Her breath hitched. This wasn't supposed to happen.

In every other instance, she had been a silent observer, watching history unfold like a scene from a movie. But now, Aarav's dark eyes were fixed on hers, his expression shifting from confusion to something deeper—**recognition.**

"Who are you?" Aarav's voice was soft, but there was an edge to it, a wary curiosity.

Meera followed his gaze, her brows furrowing as she looked at Anika. But there was no fear, no shock—just a strange sense of **understanding**, as if she, too, felt something familiar about this moment.

Anika tried to speak, but her throat was dry.

Could they really see her? Could they hear her?

Time had never acknowledged her presence before.

A sudden wave of dizziness crashed over her. The room began to blur, the warm glow of the oil lamps fading into darkness. The voices of Aarav and Meera **echoed and distorted**, like words lost in the wind.

And then, just as suddenly as it had begun, the pull of time **released her**.

Back to the Present

Anika gasped as she **snapped back into reality**.

She was sitting in the same old study, but everything was different again—the air was cold, the walls were cracked, the letters were scattered before her.

Her hands trembled as she clutched the edge of the desk, her heart racing.

They had **seen her**.

For the first time, she hadn't just witnessed history—she had **become a part of it**.

What did this mean? Was she rewriting the past? Was she somehow connected to Aarav and Meera in ways she couldn't understand?

The questions **swirled in her mind**, but one thing was clear.

The past was no longer just showing itself to her.

It was **calling her back.**

Echoes of the Unfinished Past

Anika struggles to come to terms with what just happened. Unlike before, when she was merely an observer, this time, Aarav had seen her. A part of history had acknowledged her presence, breaking the fragile barrier between past and present. What did this mean? Was she destined to be part of their story? As she searches for answers, the old haveli seems to whisper secrets only she can hear. And before she knows it, time pulls her back again—this time, even deeper into the past.

Anika sat motionless in the dimly lit study, her pulse still racing from the shock of being seen. The worn letters lay scattered around her, their fragile edges illuminated by the moonlight filtering through the broken window.

She ran a shaky hand through her hair, trying to steady her breathing.

They saw me.

The thought repeated itself over and over in her mind, refusing to settle. The past had never acknowledged her presence before. She had always felt like a mere shadow, watching from a distance, untouched by time. But this—

this was different. Aarav's dark, questioning gaze still burned in her memory.

She reached for the bundle of letters, her fingers brushing over the aged paper as if searching for an explanation. If she could find something, anything, to make sense of what had happened—

A sudden gust of wind **rushed through the room**, sending the letters flying into the air. Anika gasped, scrambling to catch them, but one particular letter slipped past her grasp and **floated towards the floor, landing near her feet.**

Something about it felt different.

The paper was **older**, more fragile than the others, its ink faded yet still readable.

With a deep breath, Anika picked it up and unfolded it carefully.

A Letter from the Past

"Meera, my love,"

"I do not know what the future holds for us. Every day, the world pulls us apart, forcing us into choices we do not wish to make. But I need you to know—no matter what happens, no matter how cruel fate may be—I will find my way back to you."

"Even if time itself stands in our way."

"Yours, always,"
"Aarav."

Anika's hands trembled as she read the letter.

The words felt alive, **as if they had been waiting for her to find them**. There was something eerily familiar about them, a weight in the way they were written—as if Aarav hadn't just been speaking to Meera.

As if, somehow, he had been speaking to **her**.

Her eyes darted to the date at the top of the letter—**March 5, 1925.**

Her breath caught in her throat.

That was **tomorrow**—at least, in the past.

A chill ran down her spine. **Had she found this letter for a reason? Was this the moment that changed everything?**

A strange sensation **washed over her**, an unexplainable force tugging at the edges of her reality. The candle beside her flickered wildly, the room tilting slightly as if the world itself was shifting.

And then—

Everything **went black.**

Back to 1925: A Night of Secrets

The sound of laughter and soft music filled the air as Anika's eyes fluttered open.

She was standing in the **courtyard of the haveli**, surrounded by glowing lanterns and the gentle murmur of conversation. Women in vibrant silk sarees moved gracefully, their bangles jingling as they exchanged pleasantries. Men in traditional sherwanis stood in small groups, engaged in quiet discussions. The scent of jasmine and freshly lit diyas lingered in the warm night air.

She was in the past—**again.**

But this time, the world around her was **alive with celebration**.

Her gaze darted around, searching for familiar faces.

And then she saw them.

Aarav stood near the edge of the courtyard, dressed in a cream-colored kurta, a glass of wine in his hand. He was speaking with an older gentleman, his expression polite but distant, as if his mind was elsewhere.

Meera was seated near a fountain, her fingers tracing absentmindedly over the surface of the water. Even from a distance, Anika could sense the quiet sadness in her.

Something was wrong.

As if sensing Anika's presence, Aarav turned his head slightly.

Their eyes met.

For a split second, **his entire body went rigid**. His grip on the glass tightened, his knuckles turning white.

He recognized her.

Not just as a stranger in the crowd—but as the same woman from before. The one he had seen in his study, the one who had disappeared before his very eyes.

Anika's breath hitched. **This wasn't a coincidence.**

Aarav took a slow step forward, his eyes locked onto hers, trying to make sense of what he was seeing.

"Who are you?" he murmured, his voice barely above a whisper.

Anika opened her mouth to speak—but before she could, a voice **cut through the air**.

"Enough of these formalities," an older man announced, raising his glass. "Tonight, we celebrate! A union between two great families!"

The crowd erupted in applause.

Anika turned sharply, her heart sinking.

The older man—a wealthy merchant, from what she could gather—stood beside another gentleman who looked **far too pleased with himself**. And beside him, looking pale and shaken, was **Meera**.

Anika's stomach twisted.

This wasn't just a party.

This was **Meera's engagement.**

She was being promised to someone else.

Aarav's expression **darkened**. His grip on the glass trembled before he set it down on a nearby table, his entire posture stiff with tension.

Anika didn't need to hear the rest. She already knew.

Aarav and Meera were being **torn apart by forces beyond their control.**

And somehow, against all reason, **Anika was here to witness it.**

She felt another shift in the air—another pull, warning her that her time here was limited. But she wasn't ready to leave. **Not yet.**

She needed answers.

And for that, she needed to speak to **Aarav.**

The Silent Goodbye

Anika realizes that she has landed in a moment that changes everything—the night Meera's fate is sealed. Watching Aarav's heartbreak unfold before her eyes, she feels an urgent need to intervene, to stop what she already knows will lead to pain and separation. But how much power does she really have? And what will happen if she changes the course of history? As she searches for Aarav, time plays its tricks once again, pulling her deeper into the past, leaving her with more questions than answers.

Anika's heart pounded as she took in the scene before her. The courtyard, glowing with golden lanterns, had suddenly become a place of sorrow rather than celebration. The moment she had read about in Aarav's letters—Meera's forced engagement—was happening right in front of her.

Aarav stood still, his face unreadable, but Anika could see the storm raging behind his dark eyes. Meera, sitting quietly beside her father, looked down at her lap, her fingers clenched into fists.

She doesn't want this.

Anika's chest tightened. Meera wasn't just another name in an old letter anymore. She was real. **She was suffering.**

The merchant—Meera's father—stood before the gathering with a proud smile, his voice booming through the courtyard.

"Our families have long been tied in business," he declared, raising his glass, "and now, with this engagement, our bond will grow even stronger!"

The crowd erupted in applause. But not Aarav. Not Meera.

Aarav's hand curled into a fist at his side, his entire body stiff with tension.

Anika saw it in his eyes. The helplessness. The quiet, burning **rage** of a man who was watching the love of his life slip away from him.

She knew she shouldn't get involved. She didn't belong here. But she couldn't just stand there and watch.

Before she could think it through, her feet moved on their own, weaving through the crowd. She needed to find Aarav before he did something reckless—before the past unfolded exactly as it had before.

Aarav's Breaking Point

She found him near the edge of the courtyard, away from the laughter and music, gripping the stone railing so tightly that his knuckles had turned white.

"You're not okay," she said softly.

Aarav turned sharply, his eyes widening as he saw her. He took a hesitant step toward her, searching her face as if trying to make sense of something.

"You," he breathed. "You're real."

Anika's throat went dry. He recognized her.

He **remembered** her.

"Who are you?" Aarav asked, his voice low, cautious. "I saw you before··· in my study. And now you're here."

Anika hesitated. She couldn't tell him the truth. He wouldn't believe her.

"I—" she started, but before she could say another word, another voice interrupted them.

"Aarav," Meera's voice was barely a whisper, but it was enough to steal his attention.

Anika turned to see Meera standing a few feet away, her eyes glistening with unshed tears. For a moment, the world around them seemed to fade. It was just the three of them, trapped in a moment that had already been written in time.

"Aarav," Meera repeated, her voice shaking. "Please don't—don't do anything foolish."

Aarav exhaled sharply, his shoulders tensing. "Meera, I—"

"Promise me," she cut in, her voice urgent. "Promise me you won't ruin your life because of this."

Anika could see the weight of those words on Aarav. Meera wasn't just asking him to stay silent—she was **begging** him to let her go.

But how could he? How could he walk away from the woman he loved?

Anika knew this was the moment. The moment history had recorded. The moment where **Aarav did the hardest thing of all—he said nothing.**

His fists clenched at his sides, his jaw tightened, and then, after what felt like an eternity, he gave the smallest nod.

It was his silent goodbye.

Meera's breath hitched, but she nodded back, tears slipping down her cheeks.

And then, just like that, she turned and walked away.

Aarav didn't stop her.

He didn't run after her.

He just **stood there**, watching the love of his life disappear into a future that didn't belong to him.

The Pull of Time

Anika felt it again—the strange **pull** at the edges of her reality.

Her head grew light, her vision blurred.

No, not yet.

She tried to fight it, to stay just a little longer, but time had other plans.

The golden lights of the courtyard **faded**, replaced by the eerie silence of an abandoned haveli. The music was gone, the voices lost to history.

She was back.

Back in the present.

But this time, something was different.

The past had seen her. A man from history had looked into her eyes and remembered her.

And for the first time since it all began, Anika realized—

She wasn't just a visitor in the past anymore.

She was a **part of it.**

Echoes of the Past

Anika wakes up in the present, her heart still pounding from the events she witnessed in 1925. The echoes of Meera' s sorrow and Aarav' s silent heartbreak refuse to fade. But something has changed—Aarav saw her. He recognized her. The past is no longer untouched. As Anika struggles to make sense of what' s happening, she starts to feel an even deeper connection to the haveli, as if it is calling her back. Determined to uncover more, she searches for clues in her family' s history, but what she discovers leaves her with more questions than answers.

Anika jolted awake, gasping for breath.

The wooden floor beneath her was cold, the room around her eerily silent. The golden lanterns of the past were gone, replaced by the dim light of the modern-day haveli. The walls, cracked and worn by time, felt suffocating. She could still hear the distant echoes of Meera's voice, the pain in Aarav's eyes burned into her mind.

She sat up slowly, trying to calm herself, but her hands trembled. **This was real.** This wasn't just some vision or dream. She had been there, she had seen it all—and **Aarav had seen her.**

The very thought made her chest tighten. Had she changed something? Had her presence altered the past in ways she couldn't even begin to understand?

She pulled her knees to her chest, trying to piece it all together. The last thing she remembered before being pulled back was the way Aarav looked at her—his confusion, his curiosity. He **knew** she was there.

Could it be possible that she wasn't just an observer anymore?

The air in the room was thick with dust, but it wasn't just that. The haveli itself felt different, as if it had been disturbed by something—or someone.

She needed answers.

The Search for Truth

Anika forced herself to her feet, her legs unsteady as she moved toward the study. She had to go back. She had to understand what was happening to her.

The desk where she had first found Aarav's letters still sat in the corner, its surface covered in old papers. She flipped through them frantically, searching for anything that might tell her more about Meera and Aarav's fate.

But something else caught her eye.

A **painting.**

It had been buried beneath a pile of old fabric, forgotten with time. She carefully pulled it out, her fingers trembling as she wiped away the dust.

And then she saw him.

Aarav.

It was unmistakable. His deep, thoughtful eyes, his sharp features, the same quiet sadness that had haunted him in 1925. But there was something even more shocking—standing beside him, barely visible in the background, was a woman.

A woman who looked **exactly like her.**

Anika's breath caught in her throat.

How was this possible?

Had Aarav painted her?

Had he remembered her?

Her mind raced with questions she didn't have answers to. If this painting existed, it meant that her presence in the past had left a mark. She hadn't just been a spectator—she had become a **part of history.**

The thought sent chills down her spine.

She needed to know more.

An Unexpected Visit

Just as she was about to take another look at the painting, a sudden knock on the door made her jump.

Her heart pounded in her chest as she hesitated, then quickly placed the painting back where she found it. She took a deep breath and made her way to the door.

Standing outside was **Ishaan.**

The sight of him should have brought her comfort, but instead, she felt a strange sense of unease. Did she look as shaken as she felt? Could he tell?

"Where have you been?" Ishaan asked, his brows furrowed in concern. "I've been calling you for hours."

Anika blinked, her mind struggling to process time. Hours? Had she really been gone that long?

"I— I was just···" She trailed off, not knowing what to say. **How could she explain something she didn't even understand herself?**

Ishaan's eyes softened. "Are you okay?"

Anika wanted to say yes, to tell him everything was fine, but the words wouldn't come. Instead, she simply nodded.

Ishaan stepped closer, lowering his voice. "You look like you've seen a ghost."

If only he knew.

The Past Calls Again

That night, Anika couldn't sleep. She tossed and turned, her mind racing with everything she had discovered. The painting, Aarav's recognition, Meera's heartbreak—it was all connected. But how?

She stared at the ceiling, listening to the distant sound of the wind rustling through the old haveli. **What if she could go back?**

A part of her knew it was dangerous. She didn't belong in that time. But another part of her **needed** to see Aarav again.

She closed her eyes, taking a deep breath.

And then, just like before, the pull came.

A strange, weightless feeling washed over her, like being gently pulled by invisible hands. The room around her blurred, the sounds of the present faded—

And when she opened her eyes again, she was back.

The year was **1925.**

And this time, Aarav was waiting for her.

The Artist's Confession

Anika finds herself once again in the world of 1925, but this time, something is different. Aarav is waiting for her. He doesn't just see her—he acknowledges her presence. The lines between past and present blur further as she realizes that her existence in his time is no longer a secret. In the quiet sanctuary of his art studio, Aarav finally confronts the mystery of her presence. But as the bond between them deepens, so does the weight of the truth Anika cannot reveal.

The scent of fresh paint and aged wood filled the air as Anika's vision cleared. She was back.

This time, she was not standing in the grand courtyard of the haveli. She was in a **small, dimly lit studio**, surrounded by canvases, paintbrushes, and the lingering scent of turpentine. The flickering flame of an oil lamp cast long shadows on the walls, dancing across unfinished paintings.

And then, she saw him.

Aarav.

He was sitting at his easel, his back turned to her, his brush hovering over a canvas. But he was not painting. He was **waiting**.

He knew she would come.

Anika's breath hitched as he finally turned around, his eyes locking onto hers with an intensity that sent shivers down her spine.

"You came back," he said softly, as if he had been expecting her.

Her heart pounded in her chest. **He knows.**

Aarav's Questions

For a long moment, neither of them spoke. The silence was thick with unspoken questions, the weight of an impossible reality pressing down on both of them.

Then, Aarav set his paintbrush down and stood up, his gaze never leaving her.

"Who are you?" His voice was steady, but there was something beneath it—an edge of desperation, of curiosity, of **hope**.

Anika opened her mouth, but no words came out. How could she possibly explain? How could she tell him that she came from a future where his name was forgotten, where only his paintings and his letters remained?

"I—" she started, but Aarav stepped closer.

"I have seen you before," he said, his voice quieter now. "Not just that night in the courtyard. **Before that.**"

Anika's breath caught.

Before?

"I saw you in my study," he continued, his eyes scanning her face as if trying to piece together a puzzle. "I saw you looking at my letters. I thought I imagined it. A shadow, a trick of my mind. But then I saw you again that night."

He took another step closer.

"And now··· here you are. As real as the air I breathe."

Anika swallowed hard. **He had noticed her before she even knew she was in his world.**

The realization made her head spin.

"I don't know how to explain it," she finally admitted. "I don't know why I'm here, or how. I just··· am."

Aarav studied her for a long moment, his expression unreadable. Then, to her surprise, he **smiled.**

A sad, knowing smile.

"I should be frightened," he murmured, more to himself than to her. "But I'm not."

A Bond Across Time

Aarav turned away, moving toward the canvas he had been working on before she arrived. Anika stepped closer, her eyes drawn to the painting.

Her breath caught in her throat.

It was **her.**

Not just a vague figure resembling her—**it was her.** The way her hair fell over her shoulders, the way her eyes held secrets even she couldn't understand. **He had painted her.**

"You···" she whispered, unable to finish the sentence.

Aarav looked at her, his expression unreadable. "I don't know why, but I felt the need to capture you. Even before I truly saw you. As if··· I already knew you."

Anika's pulse quickened. **How was this possible?**

She had come here searching for answers, but the more time she spent with Aarav, the more questions she had.

"You don't belong here, do you?" Aarav's voice was quiet, careful.

Anika's breath caught.

"No," she admitted, her voice barely above a whisper. "I don't."

Something flickered in Aarav's eyes. A sadness that went deeper than she could understand.

"Then why do I feel like I've known you forever?"

Anika had no answer.

A Fateful Decision

The oil lamp flickered, casting golden light over Aarav's face, over the paintings that surrounded them. The air between them felt charged, filled with words left unspoken.

Anika wanted to tell him everything. About the future, about what would happen to him. About how his name would disappear, his love story buried in time.

But she couldn't.

She **wasn't supposed to change history.**

And yet, something deep inside her whispered that history had already changed.

Aarav had seen her before he was supposed to. He had painted her before she had ever stepped into his time.

Their destinies were intertwined in a way she couldn't explain.

And maybe, just maybe—

This wasn't the first time.

Maybe she **had been here before.**

And maybe··· she had loved him before, too.

Unfinished Letters

Anika's presence in Aarav's world deepens as she finds herself drawn into the mysteries surrounding his life. As the bond between them strengthens, Anika stumbles upon a stack of unfinished letters hidden away in his study—letters filled with emotions, confessions, and questions left unanswered. Each word on the delicate parchment carries a weight of longing, as if Aarav had been writing to someone he could never reach. But the real shock comes when she realizes that these letters—written nearly a century ago—seem to be addressed to her.

The studio was silent except for the rhythmic sound of the oil lamp crackling, casting long shadows along the wooden floor. The painting of Anika still rested on the easel, its colors raw and untouched, as if Aarav had been frozen in time, waiting for her return.

Anika swallowed hard. The more time she spent in 1925, the harder it became to ignore the pull of the past. She wasn't just observing history—she was becoming a part of it.

Aarav stood near the window, his fingers tracing patterns on the fogged-up glass. He looked deep in thought, lost in something unspoken.

"I want to show you something," he said finally, his voice barely above a whisper.

Anika looked at him in surprise, but he was already walking towards the far end of the room, where a tall wooden shelf stood covered in dust. With careful hands, he pulled out a small bundle of papers, tied together with a delicate silk ribbon.

"These···" Aarav hesitated. "These are my letters."

Anika took a slow step forward, her heart pounding.

"I never sent them," he admitted. "I never knew who they were for. But I kept writing them anyway."

Her fingers trembled as she reached for the pages, the delicate parchment aged with time. She untied the ribbon, her breath catching in her throat as her eyes scanned the words.

And then, she froze.

They were addressed to her.

Letters Across Time

The ink had faded slightly, but the words were still clear.

"To the one who lingers in my shadows, the one I see but do not know..."

Anika's pulse quickened.

"I do not know your name. I do not know if you are real or just a figment of my restless mind. But you are there—I feel you watching me, whispering in the silence."

Her breath hitched.

Aarav had written these letters **before he ever saw her in the courtyard.**

He had sensed her presence **before she ever came to 1925.**

Anika's fingers tightened around the papers. The impossible reality of her existence in his time was unraveling in ways she couldn't explain. Had she always been a part of his story? Had her presence in the past been predestined, a loop that was never meant to be broken?

Aarav watched her carefully, his expression unreadable.

"I wrote them when I felt like I was losing myself," he admitted. "There were nights I would wake up, certain that someone was there, watching over me. But when I looked··· there was no one."

Anika's throat felt dry.

"It was you, wasn't it?" he asked quietly. "You were always here."

She wanted to deny it, to tell him it wasn't possible. But the letters in her hands told a different story.

She had been here before. **Maybe she had always been here.**

The Weight of the Past

Aarav turned away, running a hand through his dark hair, frustration evident in his posture.

"I don't understand any of this," he murmured. "I don't know why I feel like I've known you forever."

Anika remained silent, her mind racing with possibilities. If Aarav had been writing to her before they even met, then that meant—

Time wasn't linear.

Her presence in his life wasn't a coincidence. It had always been a part of his story.

She looked at him, standing there against the backdrop of a world she wasn't supposed to belong to. She felt the weight of the secret she carried—the truth she could never tell him.

That one day, he would disappear from history.

That everything he was, everything he created, would be forgotten.

Her chest ached. Could she let that happen?

Could she truly return to the future knowing that his name would be lost forever?

Aarav turned back to her, his dark eyes filled with something unspoken.

“What happens now?” he asked, his voice barely above a whisper.

Anika had no answer.

All she knew was that she wasn’t ready to leave.

Not yet.

Not when she still had so many questions.

And not when she was starting to realize—

That maybe, just maybe, she was falling in love with him.

A Thread Between Worlds

Anika struggles to understand the impossible connection between her and Aarav. As the days pass in 1925, she begins to lose track of time, drawn deeper into his world. Meanwhile, Aarav becomes increasingly restless, haunted by dreams of a future he doesn' t recognize. Their bond strengthens, but with it comes the fear that time itself is slipping through their fingers. When Anika stumbles upon a portrait hidden away in a dusty corner of the haveli, she realizes that her presence in the past might not be as accidental as she once believed.

The morning light filtered through the old wooden windows of the haveli, casting golden streaks across the floor. Anika sat at Aarav's study desk, running her fingers over the fragile edges of the letters he had written.

She had spent the entire night reading them, trying to make sense of the impossible—how he had known her before they had even met. The words on those pages felt like whispers from time itself, calling her toward a fate she couldn't yet understand.

Aarav, sitting across from her, watched her closely.

"You haven't said a word since you found the letters," he finally said.

Anika looked up, meeting his gaze. "Because I don't know what to say."

He sighed, running a hand through his hair. "Neither do I. But I know that I feel like I've known you forever, Anika. And I can't explain why."

She felt her heart tighten at the way he said her name—softly, carefully, as if afraid it would disappear into thin air.

"You once told me you don't belong here," he continued. "If that's true, then where do you belong?"

Anika opened her mouth to respond, but no words came.

She couldn't tell him the truth.

Not that she was from the future.

Not that she knew his story ended in tragedy.

Not that one day, she would wake up in her own time, and he would become nothing more than a fading memory.

Instead, she stood up abruptly. "I need some air."

Aarav didn't stop her. He simply watched as she walked out of the study and into the long, winding hallways of the haveli.

A Portrait in the Shadows

The haveli was quiet, the air thick with the scent of old wood and forgotten stories. Anika wandered aimlessly, her mind clouded with questions.

Her feet carried her toward a part of the house she had never explored before—a wing covered in dust, the doors barely touched.

As she pushed open one of the heavy wooden doors, a strange feeling settled in her chest.

Inside, old paintings leaned against the walls, covered in white sheets. The smell of aged canvas filled the air. It was a forgotten storage room, abandoned for years.

And then, in the far corner, she saw it.

A portrait.

Unlike the other paintings, this one wasn't covered. It stood proudly against the wall, its colors slightly faded but still striking.

Anika stepped closer, her breath catching in her throat.

It was a painting of a woman.

A woman who looked exactly like her.

Her knees nearly gave way. The resemblance was **unmistakable**—the curve of the lips, the depth in the eyes, the way her hair fell over her shoulders.

But this portrait wasn't modern. The paint, the technique—it belonged to this time. It belonged to **Aarav's time.**

Her hands trembled as she reached out, her fingertips hovering over the surface of the painting.

Who was she?

Why did this woman look exactly like her?

Had she been here before?

Was history repeating itself?

The room suddenly felt too small, too suffocating. Anika turned on her heel and ran back toward Aarav's study, her pulse hammering in her ears.

The Weight of the Truth

Aarav was still seated at his desk when she burst into the room, breathless and shaken.

He stood up immediately. "Anika, what happened?"

She couldn't form the words. Instead, she grabbed his hand and pulled him toward the forgotten wing of the haveli.

The moment they entered, Aarav's gaze fell on the portrait.

And he **froze.**

His face paled as he stepped closer, his fingers hovering over the edge of the frame.

"This··· this was my mother's painting," he whispered.

Anika's eyes widened.

"She painted this before she passed away," Aarav continued, his voice distant, as if recalling something buried deep in his memories. "She told me once that this woman was special··· that she was someone I would meet when the time was right."

He turned to look at Anika, his expression unreadable.

"She told me that when I saw her, I would understand my destiny."

Anika felt the ground shift beneath her.

This wasn't just about the past or the future anymore.

Something bigger was at play.

A force beyond time.

And she was **right in the middle of it.**

A Bond That Defies Time

Aarav turned back to the portrait, his fingers brushing against the nameplate at the bottom of the frame.

Anika stepped closer, her breath catching as she read the engraving.

"Anika."

Her own name.

Her vision blurred as she looked up at Aarav. He was already watching her, something unspoken lingering in his eyes.

"Who are you, really?" he asked, his voice barely above a whisper.

Anika swallowed hard.

She didn't know anymore.

All she knew was that she was meant to be here.

That their story wasn't just a love story.

It was something much, much more.

Something written in the very fabric of time itself.

Echoes of a Forgotten Love

Anika and Aarav are shaken by the discovery of the portrait. The realization that her name has existed in this time long before she arrived fills her with questions. How is it possible that she was painted decades ago? As she and Aarav search for answers, they come across a hidden diary—one that belonged to Aarav’ s mother. Within its pages, they uncover a love story eerily similar to their own, revealing secrets about fate, reincarnation, and an unfinished story that has been waiting to be completed.

The nameplate on the portrait gleamed under the dim lantern light.

"Anika."

Anika stood frozen, her breath caught in her throat. She traced the delicate gold letters with her fingers, half expecting them to disappear like an illusion.

“This doesn’t make sense,” she murmured.

Aarav was silent beside her, his eyes locked onto the painting. “This was here long before we met,” he said, his voice laced with something Anika couldn’t quite place—wonder, disbelief, or maybe··· fear.

She turned to him. “You said your mother painted this?”

Aarav nodded slowly. “Yes. My mother, Devyani Sen. She was an artist, just like me. She painted this before she passed away, and she always told me that this woman—” He gestured toward the portrait. “—would change my life.”

Anika’s hands trembled. “But how? How could she have known me?”

Aarav’s eyes darkened with thought. “Maybe··· maybe she saw something we don’t understand yet.”

A silence settled between them, thick with unspoken questions.

Then, as if something clicked in his mind, Aarav turned to her suddenly. “Come with me.”

A Mother's Secrets

Aarav led her through the winding hallways of the haveli, his steps urgent, his grip firm around her wrist. They arrived at a large wooden door, different from the others—locked, untouched for years.

He reached into his pocket, pulled out a rusted key, and unlocked it. The door creaked open, revealing a small, dust-covered room.

"This was my mother's room," Aarav said softly, stepping inside.

Anika hesitated before following. The space felt untouched by time—old books, delicate sketches, and unfinished paintings lined the walls. It was as if Devyani Sen had simply left one day and never returned.

Aarav walked toward a wooden trunk in the corner and knelt beside it. His hands were careful as he lifted the lid, revealing stacks of papers, old photographs, and a single leather-bound book.

A diary.

Aarav's fingers hesitated over the cover before picking it up. He exhaled deeply, then handed it to Anika.

"This might have answers," he said.

Anika took the diary with shaking hands, opening to the first page.

The Past Speaks

The ink had faded with time, but the words were still readable.

"To the woman who will find this when the time is right… "

Anika felt her heartbeat quicken. She glanced at Aarav, who was staring at the words with equal intensity.

She continued reading.

"I have seen you in my dreams. I do not know your name, nor the time you belong to, but I know your soul. You will come when my son needs you the most. You will change his destiny, and in return, he will change yours."

Anika's fingers gripped the edges of the diary.

"This love, this story, is not new. It has happened before. It was left incomplete, unfinished by time. But now, you have a chance to finish what was once started. To rewrite the fate that was taken away."

Her breath shuddered.

Aarav's mother had known.

She had seen **her.**

And she had **known** about their love before it had even begun.

Aarav swallowed hard. “What does this mean?”

Anika looked up at him, her chest tightening.

“It means,” she whispered, “that we’ve been here before.”

A Story Left Unfinished

The rest of the diary was filled with sketches—some of Aarav as a child, others of nameless figures. But as Anika flipped through the pages, one drawing made her stop cold.

It was a sketch of **her.**

Not just someone who looked like her—**her.**

Her face, her hair, the exact way she looked now.

“This isn’t possible,” she whispered.

Aarav’s jaw tightened. “But it’s real.”

He turned to her, his dark eyes intense. “If this has happened before, then why don’t we remember?”

Anika didn’t have an answer.

But as she stared at the sketch, something in the back of her mind stirred.

A flash of something—unfamiliar, yet strangely **familiar.**

A woman in the same courtyard, standing in the same place she had stood when she first arrived.

A voice whispering a name.

A storm. A parting. A love that was never meant to end.

Her heart pounded wildly.

"I don't know how," she admitted, her voice barely above a whisper. "But I think we're reliving something that was never supposed to be forgotten."

Aarav reached for her hand. "Then we need to find out what happened. We need to know how this story ends."

Anika held onto his gaze.

But deep down, something in her told her she already knew.

It had ended before.

And if time was repeating itself…

Would it end the same way again?

Shadows of the Past

As Anika and Aarav dive deeper into the mysteries of the diary, they find unsettling connections between their present and a forgotten past. Anika begins experiencing visions—fragments of another life, another love that ended in tragedy. With each passing moment, the boundary between her world and 1925 starts to blur even more. Meanwhile, Aarav struggles to understand what fate has written for them. Are they truly in control, or are they simply reliving a love story doomed to repeat itself?

The silence between Anika and Aarav was thick with unanswered questions. The weight of the diary pressed against Anika's lap, its secrets stirring something deep within her—something she wasn't sure she was ready to face.

"This love··· this story···" she murmured, her fingers grazing the worn pages. "It happened before. But how?"

Aarav sat beside her on the floor of his mother's abandoned room, his expression unreadable. "If we've lived this before, then why don't we remember?"

Anika didn't have an answer. But something inside her whispered that memories—**real** memories—didn't just vanish. They were buried. Waiting to be uncovered.

As she ran her hand over the sketches, her vision blurred. The edges of the world around her softened, and suddenly, she wasn't in the haveli anymore.

She was **somewhere else.**

A Glimpse Into the Past

Anika blinked. The air was thick with the scent of rain, the sound of distant thunder rolling through the skies. She was standing at the entrance of the haveli—but it wasn't abandoned. It was alive. Lanterns flickered along the corridors, their warm glow illuminating the grand entrance. Servants rushed by, carrying trays of food and silk-draped fabrics. A carriage waited outside, its golden frame gleaming under the moonlight.

And then she saw **her.**

A woman dressed in an emerald green saree, her hair cascading down her back in long waves. Her face was turned away, but Anika felt an overwhelming sense of recognition—**as if she was looking at herself.**

The woman stepped forward, her voice trembling as she whispered a name.

"Aarav…"

A shadowed figure stood near the courtyard, his back turned toward her. The sound of heavy rain filled the space between them.

“Please,” the woman pleaded, stepping closer. “Don’t do this.”

The man turned, his face coming into view.

Aarav.

But he wasn’t the Aarav she knew. He was different—his eyes filled with something she couldn’t place. Pain. Sorrow. Regret.

“This isn’t our choice,” he said softly. “This is fate.”

“No.” The woman shook her head. “I don’t believe that.”

A crack of thunder split the sky. The winds howled through the open courtyard, blowing out the lanterns one by one.

The woman reached out.

But before she could touch him—before she could hold him—everything **faded.**

Waking Up in Two Worlds

Anika gasped, snapping back to the present. Her body jolted as if she had fallen from a great height. She was back in Aarav's mother's room, the diary still clutched in her hands.

Her breathing was ragged. Her skin was cold.

Aarav's worried eyes searched her face. "What happened?"

Anika swallowed hard. "I··· I saw something."

She looked around, trying to ground herself, trying to shake the eerie sensation still lingering in her bones.

Aarav leaned closer. "Saw what?"

She turned to him, her heart pounding. "Us."

Aarav stilled. "What do you mean?"

"I saw us, Aarav. In the past. In this same haveli." She pressed a hand to her temple, trying to make sense of the vision. "I was there. You were there. But it wasn't **me**—not exactly. It was someone else who looked like me. And you···" She hesitated. "You weren't the same either."

Aarav's throat bobbed as he swallowed. "What did we say?"

Anika hesitated. The emotions in the vision were still raw, as if she had actually lived through them. "We were saying goodbye."

Aarav's jaw clenched. "Then that means···"

Anika met his gaze. "We were separated."

The Fear of Repeating History

A heavy silence filled the room. The diary sat between them like a relic of unfinished destiny.

Aarav finally spoke. "If this happened before, then how did it end?"

Anika shook her head. "I don't know."

Aarav exhaled, raking a hand through his hair. "We need to find out."

Anika nodded. "But what if···" She hesitated, the weight of her next words pressing down on her. "What if we can' t change it?"

Aarav reached out, cupping her face in his hands. His touch was warm, grounding. "Then we fight," he said firmly. "We fight against whatever is trying to pull us apart."

His determination sent a shiver down her spine.

Anika wanted to believe him.

But deep down, a part of her feared that fate had already written the ending.

That no matter how hard they tried···

They would lose each other again.

The Forgotten Letter

Anika and Aarav are more determined than ever to uncover the truth about their past connection. As they dig deeper into the haveli' s secrets, Anika stumbles upon a hidden compartment in the old study room. Inside, she finds a letter—one that has been waiting to be read for almost a century. The words on the delicate, timeworn paper hold the answers they have been seeking, but they also reveal a heartbreaking truth. Could this letter be the key to breaking the cycle, or is history destined to repeat itself?

The air inside the haveli was heavy with anticipation. The walls, once silent witnesses to forgotten love, seemed to hum with the weight of untold stories. Anika and Aarav sat side by side in the dimly lit study, their fingers tracing the outlines of old books and dusty artifacts, hoping that somewhere in the past, a clue had been left behind for them.

"This place feels different," Anika whispered, running her hands over the antique desk. "Like it's hiding something."

Aarav leaned against the bookshelf, his eyes scanning the room. "If we really lived before, if this has happened before, then someone must have left a sign for us. Something that proves it wasn't just a dream."

Anika nodded, a sense of urgency coursing through her veins. She pulled open the desk drawers, one by one, finding nothing but dried-up ink bottles and fragile parchment. Then, as her fingers brushed against the wooden base of the last drawer, she felt it—**a slight gap, a hollow space beneath.**

Her heart pounded. "Aarav, help me."

Aarav rushed to her side as she pried at the false bottom of the drawer. With a small crack, the wooden panel loosened, revealing a hidden compartment. Inside, wrapped in silk, was a letter—its edges browned with age, its words almost faded into the past.

Anika carefully unfolded the delicate paper, her hands trembling. The handwriting was elegant yet hurried, as if the person writing had been desperate to capture every word before time ran out.

The Letter from the Past

"My dearest Aarav,

If you are reading this, then perhaps fate has not been as cruel as I once thought. Perhaps time, despite its merciless nature, has given us another chance.

I write this with tears staining the paper, knowing that by the time you find it, I may no longer be here. They are coming for us, my love. They do not believe that our love should exist, that a poet's daughter and a painter from the wrong class should share a destiny. I tried to fight, I tried to make them see, but love is powerless in the face of society's rules.

They will take me away before the sun rises. I do not know if I will ever see you again.

But I need you to remember one thing: Love is not bound by time. If you and I are meant to be, we will find each other again. In another life, in another time, I will search for you. And when I do, promise me you will not let me go.

Yours, always,
Meera"

A History Repeating Itself

The letter trembled in Anika's hands as she read the name at the bottom.

Meera.

She turned to Aarav, her voice barely above a whisper. "She was me."

Aarav's eyes darkened as he stared at the letter, his mind racing to piece together the puzzle of their past lives. "And I was··· him."

Everything started making sense. The visions, the emotions, the strange pull they felt toward each other—it wasn't just an unexplainable connection. It was **memories.** Pieces of a love story they had lived before. A love story that had ended in tragedy.

Anika's breath hitched. "She said they took her away. What if that's why I keep feeling this··· fear? What if the past is trying to warn us?"

Aarav clenched his fists, his jaw tightening. "Then we won't let it happen again."

But Anika wasn't so sure. The universe had already separated them once. **What if fate was stronger than love?**

The Weight of the Past

The silence between them stretched, thick with the knowledge of what they had just uncovered.

Aarav took the letter and carefully folded it back into its silk wrapping. "This letter survived a hundred years to reach us. Meera wanted us to know the truth. She wanted us to change it."

Anika looked around the haveli, the flickering candlelight casting shadows against the ancient walls. "But how? How do we fight against something we can't even see?"

Aarav reached for her hand, squeezing it tightly. "We don't have to see it. We just have to believe that love is stronger than whatever is trying to tear us apart."

Anika wanted to believe. She really did. But in the pit of her stomach, she felt it—that lingering fear, that haunting uncertainty.

What if history wasn't meant to be rewritten?

What if fate had already decided their ending?

And what if, no matter how much they fought, they were already destined to lose each other once again?

Echoes of a Promise

With the discovery of Meera' s letter, Anika and Aarav are left shaken. The truth is undeniable—history is repeating itself. But as they try to piece together what happened all those years ago, Anika starts experiencing even more vivid visions, pulling her deeper into the past. As she steps further into Meera' s world, the line between then and now begins to blur. Will she find the answers she seeks, or is she walking into a fate she cannot escape?

The room felt colder, heavier, as if the past had wrapped its fingers around the air, refusing to let go. Anika stared at the letter, its words echoing in her mind like a forgotten melody. The ink had faded, but the emotions still burned through time.

Aarav paced restlessly, his hands running through his hair. "This... this changes everything," he muttered. "Meera and I—we loved each other. And now, here we are again. Living the same story."

Anika tightened her grip on the delicate paper. "But why?" she whispered. "Why are we reliving this? What went so wrong that time itself is forcing us to come back to it?"

Aarav stopped pacing and turned to her. "Maybe we weren't supposed to be separated. Maybe this is our second chance."

Anika wanted to believe that. She wanted to hold onto the hope that love was strong enough to defy fate. But in the back of her mind, fear crept in like a slow-moving storm.

The last words of Meera's letter rang in her head: *"If you and I are meant to be, we will find each other again. And when I do, promise me you will not let me go."*

Had Aarav made that promise before? Had he failed to keep it?

Before she could dwell on it further, a wave of dizziness overtook her. The world around her blurred, the edges of reality dissolving like ink in water.

And then she was no longer in the study room.

She was in **1925.**

A Step into the Past

Anika—no, **Meera**—stood in the same haveli, but it was **alive**. The chandeliers above flickered with golden light, the walls gleamed with fresh paint, and the scent of jasmine lingered in the air. Servants bustled around, carrying silver trays filled with sweets and steaming cups of chai.

But none of it mattered. Because standing at the foot of the grand staircase was **Aarav.**

Her breath hitched. He looked the same, yet different—dressed in a crisp kurta, his eyes burning with intensity.

"Meera," he said softly, stepping closer.

A rush of emotions crashed into her. Love, longing, fear. She knew this moment. She had lived it before.

"Aarav, we have to leave," Meera said desperately. "They will come for me at sunrise. We don't have much time."

Aarav's jaw clenched. "I won't let them take you."

She reached for his hands, gripping them tightly. "Then we must go. Tonight."

But before he could answer, footsteps echoed through the haveli. A voice—a deep, authoritative voice—cut through the air like a blade.

"Meera!"

She turned, her heart pounding. Her father stood at the top of the staircase, his face twisted with anger. Behind him, men in uniforms—the British authorities.

Aarav pulled her behind him. "No. You will not take her."

"You cannot stop this," her father said coldly. "Meera belongs to a respectable family. She will marry the man we have chosen for her. This affair is over."

Meera shook her head, tears brimming in her eyes. "No, Baba, please!"

Her father's eyes hardened. "Take her."

The men stepped forward.

Aarav fought. He swung, he pushed, he yelled. But there were too many. Strong hands pulled Meera away, her screams piercing through the night.

"Aarav!" she cried, reaching for him.

He fought harder. His voice, raw and desperate, filled the air. "I will find you, Meera! No matter where they take you, I will come for you!"

The last thing she saw before darkness overtook her was Aarav being held back, his face etched with heartbreak.

Back to the Present

Anika gasped as she was yanked out of the vision. Her body jerked, her lungs desperate for air. She was back in the study room, her hands clutching the edges of the desk.

Aarav was by her side, his face filled with concern. "Anika! Are you okay?"

She looked up at him, her eyes wide with realization. "They took me away," she whispered. "That's what happened. That's why we lost each other."

Aarav knelt beside her, gripping her arms. "Who took you?"

"My father. The British. They separated us. You tried to save me, but···" Her voice broke. "You never found me again."

Aarav's hands tightened. "Then we change it."

Anika met his gaze, her heart pounding. "But what if we can't? What if it's already written?"

Aarav shook his head. "Nothing is written in stone, Anika. Not love. Not fate."

"But it was," she whispered. "Aarav··· we were meant to lose each other."

Aarav took a deep breath, his eyes burning with determination. "Then this time, we fight harder."

Anika wanted to believe him. But the echoes of Meera's past still clung to her like a shadow, whispering a truth she wasn't ready to face.

The past had already claimed them once.

And fate was watching, waiting to see if it would claim them again.

The Weight of Fate

Anika and Aarav are beginning to realize the depth of their connection to the past, but with each new vision, the truth becomes harder to ignore. Anika is torn between her love for Aarav and the fear that history is repeating itself. As she struggles to make sense of it all, the past begins bleeding into the present in ways she never imagined. Will they be able to break free from the cycle of destiny, or are they doomed to live out the same tragedy once more?

The night air was heavy, thick with the scent of rain-soaked earth and something else—something unseen but deeply felt. Anika stood by the window of the old haveli, her fingers tracing the worn wooden frame. The visions had left her shaken. Every time she thought she understood what was happening, the past pulled her deeper into its grasp, refusing to let her go.

Aarav sat across from her, his gaze unwavering. "You saw everything, didn't you?" he asked softly.

She nodded. "I was Meera. I felt everything. The fear, the helplessness··· and then nothing. Just emptiness." She turned to face him, her voice barely a whisper. "They took me away from you. You fought for me, but they were stronger."

Aarav clenched his fists, his jaw tightening. "Not this time."

Anika exhaled shakily. "Aarav, we don't know if we can change anything. What if we're just meant to go through it all over again?"

Aarav stood, stepping closer. "I refuse to believe that. If time has given us another chance, then it means we have the power to make things right. We have to try."

"But what if trying only makes it worse?" she asked, her voice laced with doubt. "What if we lose each other again?"

Aarav gently took her hands in his. "Then we fight harder. We make different choices. We don't let fate decide for us."

Anika wanted to believe him. She wanted to believe that love was stronger than destiny. But deep inside, a fear gnawed at her, whispering that history was too powerful to rewrite.

A World That Won't Let Go

As the days passed, Anika found herself slipping into the past more frequently. It no longer happened only at night or when she touched something old. Now, even the simplest things—a word, a scent, a familiar street—were enough to send her spiraling into Meera's world.

One evening, as she walked through the narrow lanes of old Kolkata, the past rushed over her like a tidal wave.

Suddenly, she wasn't Anika anymore. She was Meera. And she was **running.**

Her heart pounded as she darted through the dimly lit streets, her breath coming in ragged gasps. The sound of boots thudding against the cobbled road echoed behind her—British officers. They were chasing her.

She turned a corner and crashed into a familiar figure. Strong arms steadied her, and she looked up, her eyes meeting Aarav's.

"Meera, what's wrong?" he asked, his voice laced with concern.

"They're coming," she gasped. "We have to hide!"

Without hesitation, Aarav pulled her into the shadows of a nearby alley, pressing her against the cool stone wall. His breath was warm against her ear as he whispered, "I won't let them take you again."

But before he could move, the past began to slip away. Anika felt herself being pulled back, the scene fading like mist in the morning light.

Back in the Present

Anika stumbled, gasping for breath as she returned to the present. She was still in the streets of Kolkata, but everything was different. The old buildings now had neon signs, and cars honked in the distance. Aarav caught her before she could fall, his arms steady around her.

"What happened?" he asked urgently.

She gripped his shirt, trying to steady herself. "I was there again. I was Meera. They were chasing me, and you···" She looked up at him, her heart racing. "You were trying to save me."

Aarav's expression darkened. "This isn't just about visions anymore, is it? The past isn't just showing itself to you—it's pulling you in."

Anika swallowed hard. "And I don't know how to stop it."

Aarav brushed a strand of hair from her face. "Then we find a way. Together."

But deep down, Anika couldn't shake the feeling that the past was no longer something she was simply witnessing.

It was **living through her.**

And if she wasn't careful, it might never let her go.

Shadows Between Two Worlds

Anika' s visions are becoming more intense, leaving her drained and confused. The past is no longer just showing itself—it is pulling her deeper with each passing moment. As Aarav tries to keep her grounded in the present, Anika begins to fear that she may not be able to return one day. Meanwhile, a long-forgotten secret about Meera' s disappearance is uncovered, revealing that their love story was more tragic than they ever imagined.

Anika sat by the window of the haveli, her fingers gripping the armrest of the old wooden chair. The warm Kolkata breeze drifted in, but it did little to soothe the storm raging inside her. The visions had started taking a toll on her—each time she slipped into Meera's world, it felt harder to come back.

Aarav sat across from her, his gaze filled with worry. "You're pale," he said, leaning forward. "You barely ate today. Anika, this isn't normal."

She closed her eyes for a brief moment before whispering, "I don't think I belong to this time anymore, Aarav."

His expression tightened. "Don't say that. You're here, with me. We will figure this out."

She let out a shuddering breath. "What if we can't? What if I keep slipping away until one day, I don't come back?"

Aarav grabbed her hands firmly. "Then I will bring you back. Every single time."

The conviction in his voice was strong, but Anika could see the fear in his eyes. He was just as scared as she was.

She sighed, trying to focus on the present. "I need answers, Aarav. We have to know how Meera's story ended. I need to know what happened to her··· to us."

Aarav nodded, determination flashing in his gaze. "Then we dig deeper. We won't stop until we find the truth."

A Forgotten Truth Uncovered

They spent the next day searching through old records, speaking to local historians, and piecing together fragments of the past. Anika had already seen glimpses of Meera being taken away, but what happened after that was still a mystery.

It wasn't until they visited a dusty old library in north Kolkata that they found something—a **British police report from 1925.**

Aarav scanned the paper, his fingers gripping the fragile document. "Meera Banerjee··· arrested for attempting to escape with a rebel." His voice was tight as he continued reading. "She was taken to a confinement house··· and then···" He stopped, his hands shaking.

Anika's breath caught in her throat. "What? Aarav, what does it say?"

His eyes met hers, filled with devastation. "She was declared missing before trial. Some say she escaped. Others say···" He exhaled sharply. "She was never seen again."

Anika's blood ran cold. "Missing? No··· no, that can't be right. She wouldn't just disappear."

Aarav clenched his jaw. "There's more. A witness claimed she was taken away the night before her trial··· by an unknown man."

Anika's heart pounded. "Could it have been you?"

Aarav looked at her, his eyes filled with uncertainty. "I don't know. But we need to find out."

Slipping Through Time Again

That night, the past came for Anika once more.

As she lay on the large four-poster bed in the haveli, sleep overcame her like a silent wave. But instead of resting, she **fell.**

The world around her shifted, the air grew heavier, and suddenly—she was **Meera** again.

The cold stone walls of a dimly lit confinement cell surrounded her. A single candle flickered in the corner, casting eerie shadows on the walls. The air smelled of damp earth and something else—something metallic. **Blood.**

Meera's hands trembled as she pressed against the locked iron door. The last thing she remembered was being dragged away from Aarav. And now, she was here, alone.

But then—footsteps.

She turned sharply, her heart pounding as a shadow moved outside the iron bars. And then—**the door creaked open.**

A man stood before her, his face hidden beneath the flickering candlelight.

"Come with me," he whispered urgently.

Meera hesitated. "Who are you?"

The man stepped closer, and her breath caught in her throat. **It was Aarav.**

But something was different. His eyes··· they held an unfamiliar darkness.

"We don't have time," he said, grabbing her wrist. "You have to trust me."

Meera's heart pounded. She wanted to believe him—he was the man she loved. But something in her gut told her **this wasn't her Aarav.**

The walls began to blur again. The past was slipping away.

"Wait!" she cried. "Tell me—what happened to me?"

But before she could hear his answer, she was yanked back into the present.

Back to Reality

Anika woke up gasping, drenched in sweat. Her pulse was racing, her mind spinning. The image of Aarav—or someone who looked like him—was burned into her memory.

Aarav rushed to her side. "Anika! What happened?"

She grabbed his hands, her voice trembling. "I was there. The night she disappeared. Someone took her… and Aarav…" She swallowed hard. "It was you."

Aarav's face went pale. "What are you saying?"

Anika clutched her chest, struggling to breathe. "I don't think it was you. I think it was **someone who looked like you.** Someone she trusted."

Aarav stared at her, realization dawning in his eyes. "Then we're missing something. Someone else was involved."

Anika nodded slowly, her voice barely above a whisper. "And I think I'm about to find out who."

A Face from the Past

Anika is shaken by her latest vision. If it wasn' t Aarav who took Meera away that night, then who was it? As she and Aarav dig deeper, they uncover the existence of another man—a shadow from the past who might have been responsible for Meera' s disappearance. As Anika struggles to make sense of the past and present, she is pulled into another vision, one that reveals a terrifying truth about Meera' s fate.

Anika sat at the dining table of the haveli, staring blankly at the steaming cup of chai Aarav had placed in front of her. She didn't reach for it. Her hands were still trembling, her mind stuck in the past.

"It wasn't you," she murmured, her voice barely audible. "But it was someone who looked like you."

Aarav sat across from her, his brows knitted together in concern. "Someone Meera trusted," he repeated, trying to piece together the puzzle.

Anika exhaled sharply. "I need to go back. I need to see his face."

Aarav reached for her hands, squeezing them gently. "Not yet. We need to be careful. You've been getting weaker every time you slip into the past. What if—"

She pulled her hands away. "I don't care about what happens to me, Aarav. I need to know what happened to her. I need to know why history is repeating itself."

The room fell silent. The only sound was the soft ticking of the old grandfather clock in the corner. Anika clenched her jaw, determination burning in her eyes.

"We need to go back to the archives," she finally said. "There must be something we missed."

Aarav hesitated for a moment, then nodded. "Then let's find the truth."

A Name Hidden in History

They arrived at the old records library in the heart of Kolkata, where dust-covered books and ancient documents lay stacked in dimly lit corners. The scent of old paper filled the air as Anika and Aarav combed through historical records, searching for any mention of Meera's disappearance.

Anika flipped through a fragile notebook filled with handwritten police reports from 1925. Her fingers stopped at a name she didn't recognize. **Devraj Sen.**

She read aloud, " *'Suspected of aiding British authorities in capturing rebels. Last known location: Kolkata, 1925.' "*

Aarav frowned. "Who is he?"

Anika's heart pounded. "I don't know. But I have a feeling he's the man I saw in my vision."

She scanned the report further. Devraj Sen had been an informant—one who had betrayed revolutionaries in exchange for British protection.

A chill ran down her spine. "What if Meera wasn't just taken? What if she was betrayed?"

Aarav's fists clenched. "If this man was working with the British, then he might have had a reason to get rid of her."

Anika swallowed hard. "And he might have been the one who took her that night."

The Vision Returns

That night, Anika barely slept. She knew it was only a matter of time before the past came calling again. And when it did, she was ready.

The moment she closed her eyes, the world blurred around her.

When she opened them again, she was no longer in the haveli. She was standing in a dark alley in 1925 Kolkata. The air smelled of rain and smoke, and the streets were eerily silent.

Meera's heart was racing—no, **Anika's** heart was racing. She could feel the fear coursing through Meera's body as she turned a corner and came face to face with a man standing beneath a dim lantern.

Devraj Sen.

Anika recognized him instantly. He had Aarav's face—his sharp jawline, his deep-set eyes. But there was something cruel about his expression, something cold and calculating.

"You shouldn't have run, Meera," he said, his voice smooth but laced with warning.

Meera stepped back. "You lied to me," she whispered. "You told me you would help us."

Devraj's smile didn't reach his eyes. "I did help you," he said. "I kept you alive, didn't I?"

Meera clenched her fists. "Aarav trusted you. I trusted you."

He took a slow step toward her. "And that was your mistake."

Anika's breath hitched. This was it. This was the moment history had buried.

She had to see what happened next.

Meera turned to run, but Devraj was faster. He grabbed her wrist, pulling her close. "You belong to history now, Meera," he whispered. "And no one will ever find you."

The world spun. Anika tried to hold on, tried to see what happened next. But the past was slipping away again.

And this time, it left her with nothing but a name.

Back in the Present

Anika woke up with a sharp gasp, gripping the bedsheet beneath her. Aarav was already by her side, his eyes wide with concern.

"What did you see?" he asked urgently.

She swallowed, her throat dry. "Devraj Sen," she whispered. "He took her."

Aarav stiffened. "Are you sure?"

She nodded, her fingers tightening around the edge of the blanket. "He looked like you, Aarav. But he wasn't you."

Aarav's face darkened. "Then we need to find out what happened to him. If he took Meera··· he might be the key to everything."

Anika exhaled shakily. The pieces of the past were finally falling into place.

But the truth was still out there, waiting to be uncovered.

And this time, she wasn't going to stop until she found it.

The Man in the Shadows

Anika and Aarav now have a name—Devraj Sen. But the past isn' t always easy to trace. As they dig deeper, they uncover fragments of history that were meant to stay hidden. Who was Devraj Sen, and why did he betray Meera? The search for answers leads them to a forgotten mansion, where echoes of the past refuse to fade. And just when Anika thinks she' s close to the truth, the past pulls her back in—this time, more forcefully than ever before.

The name **Devraj Sen** lingered in the air like a curse. Anika could still hear the way he had whispered Meera's name in her vision, the way his cold fingers had gripped her wrist. The memory made her shudder.

Aarav sat beside her, scrolling through old records on his laptop. They had spent the entire morning searching for any mention of Devraj Sen, but the name had been buried under layers of history. There was barely a trace of him in the archives, as if someone had tried to erase him from existence.

"He was working with the British," Aarav said, rubbing his temples. "But there's no record of what happened to him after 1925. It's like he vanished."

Anika tapped her fingers against the table. "People like him don't just vanish. They either die in silence or live in shadows."

Aarav looked up. "Then we need to find his shadow."

The Forgotten Mansion

Their search led them to an old government record office, where yellowed files and dust-covered books held secrets no one had bothered to revisit. A kind elderly clerk, after much convincing, helped them find land records from 1925.

Anika's heart skipped a beat when she saw it—**Devraj Sen's name** attached to an old mansion on the outskirts of Kolkata.

"Sen Mansion," she read aloud. "Abandoned since 1930."

Aarav leaned in. "If that house still exists, we need to go there."

The thought sent a shiver down her spine. But if the truth was buried inside those walls, she had no choice.

That evening, as the sun dipped below the horizon, Anika and Aarav arrived at **Sen Mansion**.

The house stood like a ghost from another time—its once-grand pillars now cracked, its windows shattered, its gates rusted shut. Vines curled around its walls, as if nature itself was trying to swallow the past.

Aarav pushed the creaky gate open, and they stepped inside.

Dust swirled in the air as they walked through the foyer, their footsteps echoing in the emptiness. Paintings of forgotten ancestors hung on the walls, their eyes following them as if they knew their secrets were about to be uncovered.

Anika ran her fingers over a wooden table, brushing away years of dust. A faded portrait lay beneath it—a man with sharp features, deep-set eyes, and an uncanny resemblance to Aarav.

"Devraj," she whispered.

Aarav's jaw tightened. "This is the man who betrayed Meera."

A creaking sound echoed from the hallway. Anika turned sharply. "Did you hear that?"

Aarav nodded. "We're not alone here."

They moved cautiously toward the noise, stepping past broken furniture and fallen chandeliers. At the end of the hall, a door stood slightly ajar. Anika hesitated before pushing it open.

Inside, the air was thick with the scent of old books and something else—something decayed. A large wooden desk sat in the center of the room, covered in yellowed papers.

Anika reached for one. The ink had faded, but the words still sent a chill down her spine.

"Meera knows. She must be stopped."

Her breath hitched. "Aarav, look at this."

Aarav read the note, his face darkening. "He planned it. He planned to betray her."

Anika's hands trembled as she flipped through more papers. Letters. Contracts. Evidence of Devraj's deals with the British. And then, in the very last page of a leather-bound journal, she found it.

A single line, written in hurried handwriting:

"She will not leave this house alive."

Anika gasped. "Oh my God··· he killed her."

A sudden gust of wind blew through the room, scattering the papers to the floor. The temperature seemed to drop, and a strange pressure filled the air, making it hard to breathe.

Aarav grabbed her hand. "Anika, we need to get out of here."

But it was too late.

The moment Anika turned toward the door, everything went black.

The Past Calls Again

When she opened her eyes, she wasn't in the mansion anymore. She was back in 1925.

It was raining. Thunder rumbled in the distance as Meera ran through the hallways of the same house, her bare feet slipping on the polished floor.

"Meera!" a voice roared behind her.

She turned, her chest heaving. **Devraj stood at the top of the staircase, watching her like a predator.**

"You should have listened to me," he said, descending the steps slowly. "But now, it's too late."

Meera backed away. "Aarav will find me."

Devraj chuckled darkly. "By the time he does, you'll be nothing but a memory."

Anika—trapped inside Meera's body—felt the fear, the helplessness. She tried to move, but it wasn't her own will controlling her anymore. She was only a witness.

Devraj lunged forward, grabbing Meera by the wrist. She struggled, but he was stronger. He dragged her toward the locked door at the end of the hallway.

"No!" Meera screamed. "Let me go!"

Devraj yanked the door open and shoved her inside. The room was dark, cold, and filled with the scent of damp earth.

Then Anika saw it—the hole in the ground. A deep pit, dug into the floor.

Devraj stepped back, wiping his hands. "No one will ever find you here, Meera."

The door slammed shut.

And then—darkness.

Back to Reality

Anika jolted awake with a strangled gasp, her body drenched in sweat. Aarav was shaking her, his voice frantic.

"Anika! What happened? What did you see?"

She clutched his arms, her breaths ragged. "She didn't disappear, Aarav," she whispered. "She was buried. Right here, in this house."

Aarav's eyes widened. "Are you saying—"

Anika nodded, her heart pounding. "We need to find her. Meera's body··· it's still here."

The past was no longer just a story.

It was real. And it was waiting to be uncovered.

Buried Secrets

Anika' s terrifying vision has revealed the truth—Meera was never lost, never disappeared. She was buried within the walls of Sen Mansion, her story silenced by betrayal. But now, history is demanding to be rewritten. Anika and Aarav must unearth the past, quite literally, to find Meera' s remains and bring justice to a love story that was never meant to end in tragedy. However, as they dig deeper—both into the mansion and its secrets—they realize that some ghosts refuse to rest.

The silence after Anika's words was deafening.

Aarav stared at her, his mind struggling to grasp what she had just said. "Meera's body··· is still here?"

Anika nodded, still catching her breath. "Devraj killed her and buried her inside this mansion. I saw it happen."

Aarav ran a hand through his hair. "We have to find her."

The weight of those words settled heavily between them. It wasn't just about history anymore—it was about giving Meera the justice she never got.

But where could she be?

The Search Begins

They scoured the room where Anika had seen Meera's last moments. Dust coated the wooden floor, and the air was thick with an eerie stillness.

"She was locked inside here," Anika murmured, pressing her hand against the wall. "Devraj said no one would ever find her."

Aarav walked around, tapping his knuckles against the walls, listening for a hollow sound. "If he buried her here, there must be a sign."

Then, a loose floorboard creaked beneath Anika's foot.

She froze. "Aarav··· I think this is it."

Aarav grabbed a rusted iron rod from the corner and wedged it beneath the plank, pushing with all his strength. The wood groaned before finally giving way, revealing a gaping hole beneath.

A cold gust of air rushed past them. The stench of damp earth and something far older filled their nostrils.

Anika covered her mouth. "This is it."

Aarav shone his flashlight into the darkness below. The beam illuminated what lay beneath—**fragments of old fabric, bones barely visible under decades of dust, and a rusted anklet peeking out from the soil.**

Anika gasped, her heart pounding in her chest. "Meera."

Her name trembled in the air, and for a moment, it felt as if the house itself was listening.

A Soul That Still Lingers

The realization hit Anika like a wave. Meera had been crying for help all this time. Every vision, every time slip—she had been guiding her to this very moment.

Aarav's grip tightened on her wrist. "We need to call the authorities."

Anika hesitated. "But··· what if they don't believe us?"

He exhaled sharply. "We have proof. The body, the documents we found about Devraj's betrayal. This isn't just a legend anymore. It's real."

Anika nodded. They couldn't keep this hidden. Meera deserved to be found.

But before they could move, the temperature in the room dropped suddenly. The air grew heavy, pressing down on their chests. The candle on the table flickered violently, as if an unseen force had brushed past it.

And then—a whisper.

Soft. Heartbreaking.

"Thank you···"

Anika's breath hitched. "Did you hear that?"

Aarav's fingers dug into her palm. "I did."

The whisper carried through the room, and for a moment, Anika swore she could see a faint figure standing by the door—dressed in an old red saree, her eyes filled with something between sorrow and relief.

Meera.

Tears welled in Anika's eyes. "She's free now, isn't she?"

The figure didn't respond. But as the light flickered once more, Anika felt the weight of the past finally begin to lift.

Justice was coming.

Breaking the Silence

By the time the authorities arrived, dawn was breaking over Kolkata. The mansion stood as it always had—silent, ancient, forgotten.

But now, it would no longer be just a ruin. It would be remembered as the place where Meera's truth was uncovered.

The police officers listened intently as Anika and Aarav narrated everything—from the old documents to Anika's strange visions. Though skeptical at first, the discovery of human remains beneath the floor changed everything.

"This case will be reopened," one officer confirmed. "We' ll look into the records of Devraj Sen."

Aarav nodded. "He betrayed not just Meera, but history itself."

As the excavation team carefully began retrieving the remains, Anika stood at the edge of the room, watching in silence. She thought of Meera's poetry, of the letters she had written to Aarav, of the love that had been torn apart by greed and cruelty.

She reached into her pocket and pulled out Meera's last letter—the one she had found in the haveli all those weeks ago.

In faded ink, Meera's final words to Aarav read:

"Even if time separates us, even if the world stands between us, our love will never fade. It will whisper through eternity."

Anika held the letter close to her chest.

"Rest now, Meera," she whispered. "Your story will never be forgotten."

And for the first time since she had stepped into this haunting journey, Anika felt at peace.

Shadows of the Past

With Meera' s truth finally revealed, Anika and Aarav feel a momentary sense of victory. But history is never just about one story—it is a web of forgotten voices and untold secrets. As Anika delves deeper into the records of the Sen family, she realizes that Meera' s tragedy was not an isolated incident. More questions arise: What happened to Devraj Sen after Meera' s death? Why was Aarav' s name erased from history? As the past pulls her further in, Anika finds herself walking the thin line between reality and illusion—where every shadow holds a story waiting to be uncovered.

The air inside Sen Mansion was heavy with silence. Even after the authorities left, Anika and Aarav remained in the room where Meera had spent her final moments. It no longer felt like just an old ruin—it was a monument to a love that had fought against time itself.

Aarav sat on the edge of a wooden chair, staring at the place where Meera's remains had been found. "She's free now," he said softly.

Anika nodded, but a deep unease settled in her chest. "Then why do I feel like this isn't over?"

Aarav looked at her, his brow furrowing. "What do you mean?"

She hesitated before speaking. "Meera was betrayed. But what about you, Aarav? I've searched through every historical record, every mention of the Sen family, but your name doesn't exist anywhere. It's as if you were erased from history."

Aarav's expression darkened. "Devraj was powerful. He had the influence to rewrite narratives. But why would he go to such lengths?"

Anika took a deep breath. "I need to find out."

A Lost History

The next morning, Anika visited the old archives in Kolkata's National Library. The records were fragile, worn with age, their ink fading into oblivion.

She ran her fingers along the yellowed pages, searching for anything related to Devraj Sen and Aarav. The librarian, an elderly man with thick glasses, watched her with curiosity.

"You're searching for the Sen family?" he asked.

Anika nodded. "Yes. Specifically, a man named Aarav. He was a painter in the 1920s."

The librarian adjusted his glasses. "Strange··· the Sen family was quite influential in colonial Bengal. But there are very few records about them. Almost as if someone wanted to erase their past."

Anika's pulse quickened. "Do you have anything left from that time?"

The librarian sighed, then gestured to a dusty shelf in the corner. "There's a restricted section with some unsorted documents from that period. You may find something there."

Anika thanked him and hurried to the shelf. As she sifted through the old files, she felt her heart race.

Then, she found it.

A brittle newspaper clipping dated **1926.**

She carefully unfolded it, scanning the ink-stained words.

"Renowned Painter Aarav Mukherjee Missing. Last seen near Sen Mansion. Authorities declare him dead after months of search."

Anika's breath hitched.

Missing? Declared dead?

She turned to Aarav, who stood beside her, his eyes locked onto the paper. "They covered up your disappearance."

Aarav clenched his fists. "Devraj."

The past was darker than they had imagined.

The Mansion's Final Secret

Determined to uncover the full truth, Anika and Aarav returned to Sen Mansion that night. The air was thick with humidity, and the moonlight cast eerie shadows against the walls.

"Meera was silenced here," Anika whispered. "But I don't think she was the only one."

Aarav ran his fingers over the walls, his jaw tight with emotion. "Devraj wouldn't have just let me go. He must have done something."

They searched through the forgotten corners of the house, stepping carefully over creaking floorboards and dust-covered furniture. Then, in Devraj's old study, Anika noticed something—a small wooden cabinet with an intricate lock.

She tugged at the handle. "It won't open."

Aarav knelt beside her. "If Devraj hid something, it would be here."

With one swift push, Aarav forced the lock open. The cabinet door swung wide, revealing a stack of letters, a faded photograph, and an old journal with Devraj Sen's initials engraved on the cover.

Anika's hands trembled as she picked up the journal.

She flipped through the pages, her eyes widening with every word.

Devraj's confession was written in ink that had long since faded, but the weight of his words remained strong.

"Aarav Mukherjee refused my offer. He chose love over wealth, over power. I could not allow such disobedience. I arranged for his disappearance. The river holds many secrets. No one will question another lost artist."

Anika's stomach turned. "He had you killed," she whispered. "Your body was never found because··· because he made sure no one would look for you."

Aarav exhaled slowly, his face unreadable. "So that's how my story ended."

Anika reached for the photograph in the cabinet. It was of Devraj, standing proudly in front of the mansion—his face smug, victorious. The very man who had erased two lives.

But history had a way of correcting itself.

Anika clenched the journal in her hands. "We're taking this to the authorities. Devraj's crimes won't stay buried."

Aarav nodded. "It's time for the truth to be known."

Justice Beyond Time

As dawn broke over Kolkata, Anika stood outside the mansion, watching as the first rays of sunlight touched the old walls.

She knew this was only the beginning. The truth about Meera and Aarav would finally be known, their love story no longer hidden in the shadows of history.

She turned to Aarav, who looked at the rising sun with quiet reverence. "What happens now?" she asked.

Aarav smiled softly. "Now, I can rest."

Anika's chest tightened. "You mean—?"

Aarav reached out, brushing a strand of hair from her face. "Thank you, Anika. For bringing me back. For finding the truth. But my time here is ending."

A tear slipped down Anika's cheek. "I don't want you to go."

Aarav's gaze held hers, full of warmth, full of love. "We were never meant to exist in the same time. But you found me. And I will always be with you."

A golden light shimmered around him, soft and peaceful. As the morning breeze swept through the ruins, Aarav faded—his presence lingering in the air, in the whispers of the mansion, in the echoes of a love that defied time itself.

Anika closed her eyes, holding onto the warmth of his final touch.

She would tell their story.

She would make sure history remembered.

And in the quiet of Sen Mansion, she heard it one last time—**the soft murmur of a painter's brush, the gentle hum of a poet's verse.**

Love, beyond time.

Echoes of a Love Lost

With Aarav' s truth finally revealed, Anika faces the weight of what she has uncovered. The history books never spoke of him, and now she understands why—his love for Meera had cost him his life at the hands of Devraj Sen. But even though justice has been found in words, Anika is left with an emptiness she never expected. Aarav is gone. The past has finally settled, but at what cost? As she struggles to come to terms with losing him, fate delivers an unexpected message—one that makes her question whether love ever truly disappears.

Anika had never felt so alone.

She stood in the middle of the Sen Mansion's great hall, the journal clutched tightly in her hands. The morning sun seeped through the broken windows, casting golden rays on the dust-covered floor. The house was silent—eerily so. No more whispers of the past, no more fleeting glances of Aarav in the corners of her vision. The air felt hollow, empty, as if something—someone—had truly left forever.

Her heart ached.

The past few weeks had felt like a dream, a whirlwind of history, love, and mystery unraveling before her eyes.

And now it was over. Aarav was gone. Meera was free. The truth had been told.

So why did it still feel so incomplete?

She sank onto the floor, her hands trembling as she turned the pages of Devraj's journal. The ink had faded, but the words still burned into her mind. Aarav had been erased from history, his existence wiped away by power and cruelty.

"He did not deserve to be forgotten," Anika whispered, her voice breaking.

Tears welled up in her eyes. How cruel was fate, to let her find him, to let her love him, only to take him away?

A Legacy Restored

Determined not to let Aarav's name disappear again, Anika spent the next few days ensuring that his story would be known.

She took Devraj's journal, along with the letters and photographs, to the local heritage board. At first, they looked at her with skepticism—why would they reopen an old chapter of history? But when she showed them the hidden records, the forgotten evidence, the truth they had never known, their expressions changed.

"This is··· unbelievable," one of the historians murmured, holding up a sketch of Meera that Aarav had drawn.

Anika nodded. "His name was Aarav Mukherjee. He was a painter, a lover, a man who was taken from this world too soon. His love story deserves to be told."

Days turned into weeks. Articles were written, research was conducted, and Aarav's paintings—once lost in time—were finally given the recognition they deserved. His name, once erased, was restored.

His story, once hidden, was now told.

And yet, no amount of recognition could fill the void inside Anika's heart.

A Final Message

It was a cold evening when Anika found herself standing in front of an old art gallery in Kolkata. The city buzzed around her, unaware of the storm inside her heart. The exhibition inside was dedicated to "Forgotten Artists of

Colonial India," and among the displays, Aarav Mukherjee's name was finally written in bold letters.

She walked inside slowly, her eyes scanning the room. And then she saw it—one of Aarav's last paintings.

It was of a woman.

A woman with long, dark hair, standing near a balcony with her back to the viewer, looking out at the stars.

Anika's breath caught in her throat.

It was her.

Not Meera. **Her.**

Her hands shook as she read the small plaque beneath it.

"The Woman Beyond Time – By Aarav Mukherjee, 1925."

Her head spun. How? This painting was nearly a hundred years old. She had never been here before. She had never stood on any balcony like this. And yet, the resemblance was undeniable.

A soft gasp escaped her lips.

Had he known? Had he seen her even before she came into his life? Was their love truly written in the stars?

Tears blurred her vision as she reached out, her fingers barely brushing the frame.

Somewhere, deep inside her soul, she felt it—**Aarav was still with her.**

A presence. A whisper in the wind. A love beyond time.

And as she stood there, staring at the proof of their impossible connection, she smiled through her tears.

Because now, she knew the truth.

Some loves never fade.

Some souls always find their way back.

Even across time itself.

Shadows of the Past, Lights of the Future

Anika has uncovered the truth and ensured that Aarav' s name is restored in history, but the emptiness in her heart remains. The past no longer calls her back, and the visions of Aarav have faded. Yet, fate has one final thread to weave—a message hidden in time, waiting for her to find. As she walks the line between history and destiny, she is faced with the ultimate question: Was she meant to change the past, or was she always meant to remember it?

The cold air of Kolkata wrapped around Anika as she stood in front of the gallery, staring at the painting that had shaken her soul. Aarav had painted her in 1925—a time when she had not even been born. And yet, there she was, captured in his strokes, waiting in time.

She had never felt this kind of ache before.

Even after everything, after proving Aarav's existence, after bringing his love story to light, after standing before his paintings displayed for the world—she still felt like she had lost something irreplaceable.

She wanted to see him again.

Not in a painting. Not in a dream. But in the way she had seen him in the past—smiling, eyes full of passion, hands stained with paint as he spoke of art and love.

But maybe··· that was the cruelest truth of time.

You can touch the past. You can change its course. But you can never truly hold onto it.

The Last Letter

The next morning, Anika walked through the old lanes of North Kolkata, letting her feet guide her. She had no destination in mind, but something deep inside her told her to keep moving.

As she turned a corner near an old bookstore, a familiar voice called out to her.

"Beta, ek minute idhar aana." (Child, come here for a moment.)

Anika looked up to see an elderly man sitting on a wooden bench outside the store. He was the shopkeeper, someone she had met a few times while researching the mansion. His eyes were kind, lined with years of stories.

"There was a package left here for you," he said, handing her a small, dusty envelope.

Anika frowned. "For me? Who left it?"

The old man simply smiled. "Some things are not meant to be questioned. Only understood."

Confused, Anika took the envelope and carefully opened it. Inside, she found an aged, yellowed piece of paper.

Her hands trembled as she read the words.

"Anika,
If you are reading this, it means you have found the truth.
It means you have seen me, just as I have always seen you.
I do not know how, or why, but I have felt your presence
in every stroke of my brush, in every whisper of the wind.
I have loved a woman who exists beyond my time, and yet,
I have never once doubted that she is real.
If there is a force greater than fate, greater than time
itself, then I believe it is love. And maybe, just maybe,
love finds a way to live on, even when time stands against
it.
You were always meant to find me.
Forever,
Aarav."

Anika's breath hitched.

This wasn't possible.

This wasn't logical.

And yet, as she clutched the letter to her chest, she knew it was real.

Aarav had known. He had felt her presence long before she had ever come into his life.

Somewhere, deep inside her heart, she had always believed their love was something beyond this world.

And now, she had proof.

A New Dawn

That night, as Anika sat by the window of her small apartment, she looked up at the sky, wondering if Aarav could see her, wherever he was.

Maybe he was reborn somewhere.

Maybe he was just a memory in time.

Or maybe… he was still waiting for her, in another lifetime, in another place, where time would not be a barrier between them.

For the first time since this journey had begun, she allowed herself to smile.

Because even if she never saw Aarav again, even if time had pulled them apart, she knew one thing for sure—

Some loves never end.

Some hearts are forever bound.

And some souls will always find their way back to each other.

Even if it takes a lifetime.

The Bridge Between Two Worlds

Anika has uncovered the ultimate truth—Aarav knew about her long before she ever traveled back in time. His letter proves that love defies logic, that souls can be connected across centuries. But what does this mean for her future? As she grapples with this newfound revelation, she starts to notice strange occurrences—small, familiar moments that feel like echoes from the past. Is it just her mind playing tricks on her, or is there something more?

The days following the discovery of Aarav's letter passed in a haze. Anika found herself drifting between the present and the past, not in the way she once had—through visions or unexplained time slips—but in a much subtler, more delicate way.

It was in the way the wind carried a familiar scent of old books and paint when she walked through the streets.

In the way she would turn a corner and catch a glimpse of a silhouette that seemed so much like his, only to disappear in the crowd.

In the way she heard strains of an old melody—Meera's poetry—hummed by a stranger as she passed by.

It was as if the past hadn't let her go.

Or perhaps, she hadn't let go of the past.

A Familiar Presence

One evening, as Anika sat in a quiet café, lost in thought, she felt it again—that strange pull in her chest.

A presence.

Something unexplainable.

Her eyes flickered to the entrance just as a man walked in.

He was dressed in a simple white kurta, his dark hair slightly tousled, his sharp jawline carrying a quiet intensity. There was nothing out of the ordinary about him. And yet, Anika couldn't breathe.

Because when he turned, when his eyes met hers—

She swore she had seen those eyes before.

Aarav's eyes.

Her heart pounded. It wasn't possible. This was not 1925. This was now. The man standing before her was a stranger. But something deep inside her whispered otherwise.

He hesitated, as if sensing something too. And then, with a small, unsure smile, he walked toward her table.

"Excuse me," he said, his voice deep, steady. "I hope I'm not disturbing you, but··· have we met before?"

The air left Anika's lungs.

She didn't know how to answer that.

Because in one lifetime, she had loved him.

In another, she had lost him.

And now, here he was again, standing before her.

A bridge between two worlds.

A Love That Finds Its Way

Anika comes face to face with a stranger who looks, speaks, and feels eerily familiar. His presence shakes her, as if time itself is playing a trick on her. As they talk, strange coincidences begin to unfold, pulling her deeper into the possibility that Aarav' s soul has returned in a new life. Is this just wishful thinking, or has fate truly given them another chance?

The café felt smaller. The air heavier. Every sound around Anika faded into a distant hum as she stared at the man in front of her.

"Have we met before?" he repeated, his voice laced with quiet curiosity.

Anika's fingers trembled around her cup. She wanted to say no. That would be the logical answer. And yet, her heart screamed something else.

"I··· I don't know," she finally whispered.

The man smiled, tilting his head slightly. "Strange. Because I feel like I know you."

A chill ran down Anika's spine.

He took the seat across from her, unaware of the storm brewing inside her heart. "I'm Aarav," he said casually.

The world stopped.

Anika's breath hitched.

She must have misheard. This couldn't be happening.

"Aarav?" she echoed, barely managing to say his name.

"Yes," he chuckled. "Aarav Malhotra. My friends call me Aaru."

Anika's vision blurred. It wasn't just his name. It was the way he said it, the way he smiled—like a shadow of the past reaching out to her.

Fate was playing its final move.

Destiny's Puzzle

They talked. Slowly at first, then effortlessly, like two souls picking up a conversation from another lifetime.

Aarav Malhotra was an artist. A painter. He had grown up in Kolkata but had spent years traveling, drawn to places he couldn't explain. "Sometimes, I feel like I'm searching for something··· or someone," he admitted, stirring his coffee. "But I don't know what."

Anika's heart pounded. This couldn't be a coincidence.

"Do you believe in past lives?" she found herself asking.

Aarav looked at her curiously. "I don't know. But sometimes, I dream of places I've never been to··· faces I' ve never seen. And yet, they feel so familiar."

Anika's fingers clenched under the table. She wanted to tell him everything. About the letters. About 1925. About the Aarav who once loved a woman named Anika before time stole him away.

But how could she?

Would he believe her?

Would she scare him away?

The Final Connection

As they walked out of the café together, Anika felt the weight of a thousand emotions pressing against her chest.

The night was quiet, the streetlights casting long shadows on the pavement.

"Can I show you something?" Aarav asked suddenly.

She hesitated, then nodded.

They walked in silence until they reached a small art gallery. Aarav led her inside, flipping on the dim lights. The walls were lined with his paintings—each one filled with a haunting beauty.

But it was the painting at the center of the room that stole Anika's breath.

It was her.

Not exactly, but close enough. A woman standing by a window, lost in thought, her expression filled with longing.

"I don't know why," Aarav said quietly, standing beside her. "But I've been painting her for years. I don't even know who she is."

Anika's throat tightened.

It was happening again.

Aarav had felt her before he had even met her.

Just like the first time.

Fate had led them here, through time, through loss, through an unbreakable bond.

Anika turned to him, her eyes shining. "What if I told you that you do know her?"

Aarav looked at her, his brow furrowing. "What do you mean?"

She took a deep breath.

Maybe this was her second chance.

Maybe love really did find its way.

And maybe, just maybe—this time, she wouldn't lose him again.

The Echoes of Forever

Anika stands at the edge of a truth too unbelievable to speak yet too powerful to ignore. Aarav has returned—not as a ghost, not as a memory, but as a man in this lifetime. As she finally gathers the courage to tell him everything, she must face the most terrifying question of all: Will he believe her? And if he does, will he feel the same way he once did, across the distance of time itself?

Anika had never been more afraid in her life.

She stood in Aarav's art studio, her gaze fixed on the painting of the woman by the window—her reflection in colors and strokes, captured by the hands of a man who had loved her in another century.

Aarav waited, his dark eyes searching hers for an explanation.

She had spent so long trying to understand how fate had woven their souls together across time. Now, with him standing before her, she had no choice but to tell him everything.

"Do you believe in destiny, Aarav?" she finally asked, her voice barely above a whisper.

He leaned against the table, thoughtful. "I believe some things are meant to be," he said. "But I also believe we make our own choices."

Anika swallowed hard. "What if I told you we have met before? That you and I··· we knew each other in another life?"

Aarav chuckled softly, as if she were joking. "Like reincarnation?"

She nodded. "Yes. Exactly like that."

His smile faded at the seriousness in her voice. "Anika··· "

She took a deep breath. "You were a painter. In 1925. You lived in Kolkata. And you loved a woman··· a woman who looked exactly like me."

Aarav's body stiffened.

"I know how crazy it sounds," she continued, her hands trembling. "But it's true. I found your letters. Your paintings. I saw you, Aarav. I was there. I don't know how, but I was there."

His face was unreadable.

"I remember everything," she whispered. "Do you?"

Truth or Madness?

Silence stretched between them, thick and suffocating.

Aarav ran a hand through his hair, exhaling sharply. "Anika··· this isn't—this can't be real."

Her heart clenched. "It is."

"How?" His voice was raw, shaken. "How could I have lived another life? How could I have loved you before now?"

"You've felt it, haven't you?" she pressed. "That pull? Those dreams? The way you've painted me without knowing who I was?"

Aarav's jaw tightened.

"You said you've been searching for something," she continued. "Maybe you were searching for me."

He took a step back, shaking his head. "I don't—this doesn't make sense."

Tears burned in her eyes. "Neither does love that never dies, but here we are."

He turned away, gripping the edge of the table like he needed to steady himself. "I need time."

Anika felt her heart crack, but she nodded. "I understand."

She turned to leave, her fingers hovering over the door handle.

"Anika," he called softly.

She turned.

His eyes, filled with turmoil and something deeper—something buried—held her in place.

"If what you're saying is true··· if we really did love each other once···" His voice was barely audible. "Then why did I forget?"

She swallowed the lump in her throat. "Maybe you didn't."

She left him standing there, the weight of centuries pressing between them.

A Choice Across Time

The days passed in unbearable silence.

Anika waited, hoping, but she didn't push. If Aarav was truly the same soul reborn, then he had to find the truth on his own.

And then, one evening, she received a message.

"Meet me where it all began."

Her heart raced. She knew exactly where.

That night, she stood before the abandoned haveli, the place where her journey had begun. The moonlight bathed the old walls in silver, the whispers of time swirling in the wind.

Footsteps approached.

Aarav stood before her, his expression unreadable.

Without a word, he reached into his bag and pulled out a folded piece of paper—yellowed, old, fragile.

Anika gasped.

One of his letters. The same ones she had found in the hidden room.

"I went back to the library," he said quietly. "To the archives. To the place where you said I had written them." His voice trembled. "I found this."

Anika covered her mouth, tears spilling down her cheeks.

"You were telling the truth," he whispered.

She nodded, unable to speak.

Aarav exhaled shakily. "I don't remember everything··· but when I read this, I felt something. It was like a memory just out of reach."

He took a step closer, his fingers brushing hers. "I don't know how. I don't know why. But I believe you."

Anika sobbed, the weight of lifetimes lifting from her chest.

"And if I loved you once," he murmured, cupping her face, "then I will love you again."

She closed her eyes as his lips met hers, the past and present colliding, two souls finding their way back to each other.

Their love had defied time.

And now, in this life, they were finally free to live it.

Epilogue

Years passed, but some things remained eternal.

Anika and Aarav's love story, once lost in the pages of time, had finally found its way into the present. Their lives intertwined in ways neither of them could explain, but neither of them questioned it anymore. Fate had given them another chance, and this time, they were not going to let it slip away.

The old haveli in Kolkata had long been abandoned, but one evening, Anika and Aarav returned. The grand structure stood silently under the golden hues of the setting sun, its walls carrying the echoes of forgotten whispers. Hand in hand, they stepped inside, breathing in the scent of history, of love that had once flourished here.

Aarav touched the worn wooden banister of the staircase, a distant look in his eyes. "It feels like home," he murmured.

Anika smiled softly. "Because it was."

She led him to the hidden room, the place where she had first found his letters, where she had first realized their connection. The dust had settled over time, but the magic still lingered. As they stood in the dim glow of the evening light filtering through the cracked windows, Aarav reached into his bag and pulled out a small, leather-bound notebook.

"For us," he said simply.

Anika took it with trembling hands, flipping through the pages. It was a collection of their story—his paintings, her words, fragments of their past and present woven together. Their love, preserved.

"Every story deserves an ending," he whispered. "But I don't want ours to ever end."

Tears welled up in Anika's eyes as she embraced him. "It won't. Not in this life. Not in any life."

And as they stood there, wrapped in the warmth of each other, the past no longer haunted them—it simply existed, a gentle reminder that love, when true, never fades. It transcends time, generations, and even lifetimes.

Somewhere in the echoes of history, a painter had once loved a poet.

And in the present, a man had found his love again.

A love beyond time.

The End.

Summary of Love Beyond Time

Love Beyond Time is a touching story about love that never fades, no matter how many years pass. It follows the journey of Anika, a historian in modern-day Kolkata, and Aarav, a painter from 1925. The story begins when Anika finds old love letters in her family's abandoned haveli. These letters, written by Aarav, connect her to a past life she never imagined she had. As she reads the letters, she discovers that Aarav's love for a poet named Meera was deep, but their love was never meant to be.

The adventure begins with **The Forgotten Haveli**, where Anika finds the old letters. This discovery leads her into a deep mystery—**The Letter from the Past**—which takes her on a journey to uncover the secrets of a love lost in time. Anika's life starts to change as she experiences strange feelings and dreams of 1925, a time she never lived in. As **The Mystery Deepens**, she realizes that the story of Aarav and Meera is tied to her own fate.

In **A Glimpse of the Past**, Anika starts having strange visions of the past, feeling as though she is living Aarav and Meera's story. These glimpses grow stronger, and she begins to feel that she is part of something much bigger than just history. The love between Aarav and Meera was not just a story from the past—it was something that had crossed into her present life. In **Echoes of the**

Unfinished Past, Anika learns that their love was broken by a tragic end, but it never truly died.

As Anika keeps digging into the mystery, she finds **The Silent Goodbye**, the heartbreaking moment when Aarav and Meera were separated. Their love was unfinished, and those broken words would come back to haunt Anika. In **Unfinished Letters**, Anika continues to search for answers. She finds more letters that deepen the connection between her and Aarav, and in **A Thread Between Worlds**, she realizes that her soul is tied to Aarav's. Time and space don't matter in their love.

Echoes of a Forgotten Love shows how deeply Anika feels the love from the past. She begins to understand that her connection to Aarav is real, and this love has been passed down through time. As she uncovers **Shadows of the Past**, she finds out more secrets that connect her to Aarav, and she learns about the hidden parts of his life. In **The Forgotten Letter**, a letter emerges that holds the key to understanding what happened to Aarav and why his love for Meera ended so tragically.

Through **Echoes of a Promise**, Anika realizes that Aarav had made a promise to Meera to return to her, and that promise is what ties him to Anika across time. The **Weight of Fate** begins to feel heavier as Anika starts to understand the importance of the love she shares with Aarav. In **Shadows Between Two Worlds**, she faces the challenge of trying to understand how she and Aarav can be together again when the past and present seem so different.

A Face from the Past appears in Anika's life, revealing more about Aarav's true identity. She realizes that Aarav is not just a figure from history, but someone who has been reborn in the present. As **The Man in the Shadows** steps forward, the mystery behind his death and Meera's disappearance is revealed. **Buried Secrets** come to light, showing how Aarav and Meera's love was torn apart by forces beyond their control.

In **Shadows of the Past, Lights of the Future**, Anika and Aarav begin to understand their shared destiny. Their love is not just a memory; it is something that can change their future. As they move forward, **The Bridge Between Two Worlds** becomes clear. Their love is the link that connects the past and the present, and it's what will help them find happiness in this life.

Finally, in **A Love That Finds Its Way**, Anika and Aarav accept their love and choose to live their lives together, knowing that their love has crossed time and will always be with them. The story ends with **The Echoes of Forever**, showing that no matter what happens, their love will never fade. It will last through time and space, because true love never dies.

In the **Epilogue**, Anika and Aarav stand together in the haveli where their love story began. They have found each other again, and they know that their love is eternal. Time has not separated them—it has only brought them closer. They are finally together, and their love story is a reminder that love will always find a way.

Dear **Reader**,

Thank you for choosing to read *Love Beyond Time.* Your presence on this journey through time, love, and destiny means the world to me. Writing this story was a beautiful, emotional experience, and I'm so grateful that you've allowed me to share it with you.

In a world that often moves too fast, it's easy to forget that love is timeless. It crosses boundaries, heals wounds, and connects souls in ways we can't always explain. Through Anika and Aarav's story, I hope you've found the magic of love that transcends time and distance, reminding us that no matter what happens, love always finds its way.

Thank you for your time, your heart, and your support. I hope this story has touched you, just as it touched me while writing it. Every page, every chapter, every word was crafted with the deepest emotions and hope that you would feel the connection between these characters.

May love, in all its forms, continue to inspire and guide you, just as it did for Anika and Aarav.

With heartfelt thanks,
Divyam Agarwal

www.ingramcontent.com/pod-product-compliance
Ingram Content Group UK Ltd.
Pitfield, Milton Keynes, MK11 3LW, UK
UKHW021400190726
13845UKWH00028B/786

9 789334 237252